ABOUT THE AUTHOR

Gillian Lobel read English at Manchester University and then went on to become a secondary school teacher. After a long and happy teaching career, she gave it up in order to write for children instead and has become an established children's author, well-known for her touching picture books. In this, her first novel for teenagers, Gillian has tried to capture the voices of the children she used to teach, and particularly to give a voice to those with emotional and physical problems.

Gillian Lobel lives in Leicester with her husband and cats. All the children in her large, extended family keep her in touch with what it feels like to be young.

'This is Gillian Lobel's first novel for teenagers and she has a funny, appealing style that is bang-up-to-date. This book will appeal immediately to all Jacqueline Wilson fans!' *The Bookseller*

To everyone who has ever been bullied
G.L.

ORCHARD BOOKS
96 Leonard Street, London EC2A 4XD
Orchard Books Australia
32/45-51 Huntley Street, Alexandria, NSW 2015
A paperback original
ISBN 1 84362 448 6
First published in Great Britain in 2004
Text © Gillian Lobel, 2004
The right of Gillian Lobel to be identified as the author of this
work has been asserted by her in accordance with the
Copyright, Designs and Patents Act, 1988.
A CIP catalogue record for this book is available from the British Library.
1 3 5 7 9 10 8 6 4 2
Printed in Great Britain

ORCHARD BOOKS

With special thanks to:

Ellen, Emma, Jenny, Frances, Rachel, Anne,
Joseph, Tom, Danielle, the many children I taught at
St. Paul's School and Josephine Feeney,
for all her encouragement

CHAPTER ONE

Hazel Anne Mooney.

H.A.M.

Ham – Fat ham.

Mooney – Bum.

The pig.

You'd think parents would give some thought when they name their children, wouldn't you? I mean, they have this baby, this precious baby. They've waited nine whole long months for it. It's supposed to be the most wonderful thing in the world, so they give it a name that tells all the world how much they love it.

If I ever have my own baby, which seems very unlikely at the moment, I would give it a beautiful name, like Alyssa, or Jasmine, or Jessica. And I'd spend a bit of time checking out initials as well.

So why did my parents, whose surname is Mooney, christen their first child *Hazel Anne* I hear you ask? Perhaps they knew their only daughter was going to be the fattest girl in Alderman Newbold High School. Or perhaps they are just stupid.

In fact the truth is even more depressing than that. My parents were confidently expecting a boy. They were so sure I was a boy that they didn't even bother to think of a girl's name. I was going to be Dad's long-awaited centre-forward, his football star: Martin John Mooney to be exact.

In view of their disappointment, they asked the midwife what her name was. Guess what? It was Hazel Anne! Mum thought it had a nice ring, and then, Dad's sister was Hazel as well. 'Nice,' said Mum, 'nice to keep a family tradition going.'

So there you are. Fat Ham. A lovely, greasy, traditional name. I wonder if you grow up to fit your name?

Imagine the scene...

ANYTOWN MATERNITY HOSPITAL: (Mr and Mrs Mooney gaze at their firstborn child, peacefully sleeping in her little crib.)

MRS MOONEY: Oh Dave, she is so perfect!

MR MOONEY: Look at her little gold curls – she's the daughter I've always dreamed of.

MRS MOONEY: What shall we call her, darling? A name is so important!

MR MOONEY: She is so wonderful, I shall call her Miranda – Miranda Jane.

MIDWIFE: Aah!

(Close up of little Miranda's rose-petal cheeks. Her sweeping lashes open to reveal wondering blue eyes.)

Fade

Maybe – just maybe – I would have grown up to be a Miranda, tall, slim, graceful. A dancer, perhaps. Like Lauren Stevenson in our class.

Lauren. Now, there's a name! It sounds like sunlight sparkling on cool water. You'd just have to grow up beautiful with a name like that.

Lauren Stevenson is beautiful all right. Long, slim, brown legs, naturally blonde hair that looks as if she's just walked out of the hairdresser's, not a single spot on her peaches and cream complexion. And her clothes, well, it's labels all the way; you name it, she's got it. Even her school shoes are Italian designer. She's also in the top set for everything, and won the Marvin Grey award for most promising young dancer in the Midlands.

Oh yes. And she's a cow. If there was a Bovine of the Year Award, for the Most Promising Cow in the Midlands, Lauren would win that too.

I'm in set one for English and Food Technology, so those are the only times, apart from form period, Design, and PE, when Lauren and I meet – in lesson time, that is. I'm in set two for everything else, except for Maths, of course. Don't ask what set I'm in for Maths. Mrs Jessop says I have a block. If going blank and breaking out into a sweat every time you see $6y - 7 = 5y + 11$ means anything, then I have a very bad block. (Mrs Jessop says it's very simple if you approach it calmly and don't panic. I'm working on it. Honest.)

We had Food Technology today. I know a lot about food. And it's not for the reason you think, either. When you're fat everyone thinks it's because you spend your life filling your face with chocolate bars and crisps. No one ever believes me, but I don't – honestly. I'm not saying I don't have the odd bar of chocolate, but I don't stuff them like some people I could mention. Take Gillian Clarke, in our form, for example. She's got legs like an anorexic giraffe, and she's *always* stuffing herself with salt and vinegar crisps.

Dad says it's genes; we're all made that way in our family. And we all enjoy our food. Mum's always been a fantastic cook and she taught me how to cook when I was really little. *That's* why I know so much about food. My best meal is my spaghetti bolognaise. So it was a bit boring at school when we cooked our first dish – cheese on toast!

Anyway, that's why I'm in set one for Food

Tech., Tuesday, periods one and two, with Cow Features. Miss Kennedy is a really good teacher. (And she's our form teacher, too, so we see quite a lot of her.) It was theory this Tuesday, and we were doing healthy eating.

Miss Kennedy started the lesson off with a question. 'Now, 9G, I wonder if anyone can give me an example of a well-planned meal, with a good balance of the main food groups?'

Michael Evans's hand shot up.

'Yes, Michael?'

'A gigantic cheeseburger with double chips and a deep fried chocolate bar, Miss!'

Laughter.

'Very amusing, Michael. Now, a serious answer, please.'

I put up my hand.

'Yes, Hazel?'

'Jacket potato with cottage cheese and salad, followed by fresh fruit, Miss.'

'Excellent, Hazel.'

Lauren Stevenson leaned over to Amanda Brierley and whispered in her ear. It was just loud enough for me to hear, but not Miss Kennedy. 'Pity she doesn't practise what she preaches!'

They both sniggered.

I can be very good at ignoring people. When I was younger, and people started the name-calling, Dad said, 'Just ignore them; don't let them see you're upset, and then you spoil their fun.' He's right, of course, but it doesn't stop you hurting inside.

Anyway, I pretended to be checking something in my textbook so they wouldn't see I'd gone red.

'Right, everyone, I want you to finish the work you were doing last week on the most useful sources of iron in our diet. You may illustrate your work if you wish.' Miss Kennedy handed out our coursework files.

I like working on my own. I get really carried away when I'm deeply into something.

I listed all the obvious sources of iron, like eggs and liver, spinach and beef, and did some fairly OK illustrations – I'm not Leonardo Da Vinci, but I can draw so you can tell what it is. Then I thought of pork, and put that on the list. I bet Cow Features hadn't thought of pork. I was just drawing a curly tail on my pig, when Cow Features came past my table on the way to sharpen her pencil.

Suddenly she leaned across me, and grabbed

my work. She gave a snort of laughter, and danced round the table, waving my drawing over her head so everyone could see.

'Oh look, Fat Ham's drawn a beautiful self-portrait!' she cried. 'What a dear little piggy-wig, a lovely juicy little porker.'

And everybody, but everybody, heard. Michael found it so funny he fell off his seat backwards.

This time Dad's advice didn't work. I ran out of the classroom knocking over a chair on the way. Everyone saw that I was crying.

CHAPTER TWO

Behind the cycle sheds there's a muddy bank. It backs onto the railway line, and we're not supposed to go up there. Everyone does, though – it's a favourite spot for the jellyheads who think they can get away with a quiet fag. There are some overgrown blackberry bushes where you can sometimes get a bit of peace and quiet.

It was Leanne who found me. She didn't say anything, just sat down beside me and shoved a paper tissue in my hand.

'How did you know I'd be here?' I sniffed.

'You don't have to be Inspector Morse to know the best hide-out in Alderman Newbold's.'

'I feel such a fool, Leanne. Everyone heard what she said. I'm never going back into that classroom again.'

'You didn't half cause a commotion when you

ran out like that! Look, it's going to be break in a few minutes. Why don't we wait till everyone's out on the field, and creep back in by the girls' toilets?'

Leanne is my only real friend at school. She's got lots of other friends, so I don't know why she bothers with a big fat lump like me. She's clever, and she's very good at sport, too.

And she's kind.

'I'm not going back at all. I've had enough for one day. I'm going home.' I hoped Leanne wouldn't notice the wobble in my voice.

'Don't be such a nut, Hazelnut! If you do that you'll be in real trouble!'

Another thing about Leanne – she never calls me names. (OK, there's the Hazelnut joke, but it's a friendly joke – she's not laughing *at* me, and that's the difference.)

I could see she was right, so I gave my nose another blow and stood up.

'OK – you win.' I managed half a smile.

We made our way across the field, avoiding the mobiles and the Science block. Too many staring eyes there.

'You know, you have to take no notice when

people like Lauren Stevenson start bitching.'
Leanne's advice sounded all too familiar.

'It's all very well for you,' I grumbled. 'You
don't know what it's like.'

'What do you mean?' Leanne was giving me a
funny look.

'Well, look at you – you're pretty, you're in the
basketball team, you've got loads of friends.
Everyone likes you.'

'And I'm black. How would you like to be
called "Paki" and "chocolate drop"?'

I couldn't think of a thing to say. Then I found
my voice. 'I didn't know anyone ever called you
names like that,' I said stupidly. 'And you're not
from Pakistan anyway – your mum and dad
came from Jamaica, didn't they?'

'My mum was born in Birmingham and my
dad was born in Cardiff.' Leanne laughed. 'But
that doesn't make any difference to stupid people.
If you're black you get used to racist insults all
the time.'

'What, in school?'

'Not when the teachers are around – and it's
only some people. It happens a lot on the way
home from school.'

'Have you told your mum and dad about it?'

'Course I have – they get it all the time too!'

'What do they tell you to do?'

'They tell me about how it used to happen to them when they were kids, and to remember that only ignorant people talk like that. And Dad always says, "You remember, Black is Beautiful, Leanne!"'

I laughed. Leanne's dad sounded just like mine. I've got a wonderful dad – he's a bit of a softy really, like a big cuddly teddy bear – and he's always there when you need him. But I have to admit it, even he's never said Fat is Beautiful.

By this time we'd reached the back entrance to the girls' toilets. The bell still hadn't gone, so I went inside and washed my face. It looked like a bloated tomato, but I did my best with cold water and a paper towel, and in a while the scarlet faded to my usual pink. My eyes were only slightly red. You couldn't tell I'd been crying unless you looked closely.

Leanne suggested we went to the wildlife garden. It's usually quiet there.

It's one of my favourite places. There's a pond, a wild flower garden, and some picnic benches so you can sit and eat your lunch if you want to. We shared a packet of crisps.

'You know, Hazel,' said Leanne thickly, through a mouthful of crisps, 'you want to stand up for yourself more. Bullies like Lauren love it when they get you going. Next time, just give her a really hard-girl stare, and play it cool.'

'But I'm not like that, Leanne,' I faltered. 'The trouble is, I get so upset – especially when everybody laughs at me. I just don't seem to be able to help it.'

'Oh Hazelnut – everybody *didn't* laugh! I didn't, and neither did most of the other people in our class. OK, there are some prats like Michael Evans, but lots of the kids in our class really like you, you know. You just don't relax enough to see it. Besides, there's nothing to laugh at. You're fun and gorgeous – you've got such lovely hair, and your eyes are really unusual, sort of sea-green, and all sparkly!'

'Oh put a sock in it, Leanne,' I said, my cheeks flaming.

'No, I mean it, Hazel – you've got to stop putting yourself down so much!'

At that moment the corridor door opened

into the garden with a bang, and Michael Evans shot through.

'Oh hi, Leanne, have you seen an escaped piglet anywhere? Weighs fourteen stone and—'

'You bog off, Michael Evans. Ignorant pig yourself!'

Leanne was on her feet, her hands on her hips. She looked a good six inches taller than Michael. I'd never noticed before how small he is for his age.

'Ooh, temper, temper, Leanne.' He pulled a silly face. Then he went.

Suddenly I felt much better.

WADYA CALL A HAZEL
IN A HEATWAVE?
ROAST PORK!
G2GN – PAW – 24/7!
C U
L

CHAPTER THREE

Alderman Newbold High School
Spice Lane
Leicester
LW6 5QR

Dear Parents,

As you know, Alderman Newbold takes great pride in its wide range of extra-curricular activities. For some years now, we have taken advantage of the County Outdoor Pursuits Centre at Wimble Hall. We are especially proud of the tradition of our three-day Pioneer Camp for Year Nine pupils. The residential course offers the children a wide range of outdoor pursuits including abseiling, canoeing, rock climbing and orienteering. We feel that the course is not only valuable in encouraging a healthy active lifestyle, but also character building and challenging. As there is accommodation for only thirty to forty children at a time, each form group will go to the camp in turn. In order that as many students as possible may benefit from the opportunities offered by the course, we have done our best to keep costs to the minimum. The total cost for the four days is £85. This covers all food, equipment and travelling expenses. If you would like to attend the Parents' Evening on 7th September when we shall be showing a video about the camp, will you please complete the attached form and return it as soon as possible.

Yours sincerely,

A.J. Simmonds

A. J. Simmonds (Pastoral Head of Year)

This was the letter that put the finishing touches to a really horrible day. After the 'piglet' episode, I had a very quiet afternoon at school. It was obvious Miss Kennedy had given everyone a talking-to.

I know she means well and everything, but in some ways it makes it all worse.

You could tell from the way everyone was falling over backwards to be nice to me. Except Cow Features, of course. Leanne said Lauren had really got done – there had been talk of a letter home and all that. So now she really hated my guts. She kept giving me this sickly sweet smile, but the look in her eyes was pure poison.

I couldn't wait for the bell for the end of afternoon school. I read the letter on the way home. (You're not supposed to, but everyone does.) I've seen the video of last year's camp. Most people thought it was brilliant, but all I could feel was this great lump of dread, like a stone, in the pit of my stomach. Wild pictures flashed in front of my eyes. I saw this little drama unfolding in my head:

A ROCK FACE AT WIMBLE HALL: (9G line up against the skyline. Below them is a drop of thirty metres. The instructor secures a rope round Leanne, and lowers her over the edge.)

ME: *Take care, Leanne – good luck!*

LEANNE: *Bye everyone – wow, this is wicked! (Leanne skims gracefully down the rock face. Everyone cheers.)*

INSTRUCTOR: *Right, Hazel, your turn now. (He secures the rope carefully. I close my eyes. Help, somebody help! I'm a celebrity; get me out of here!)*

LAUREN: *(Sniggering to her sidekick Amanda Brierley) I wonder if they've tested the rope for a ten ton porker!*

The instructor lowers me over the edge. The rope creaks and groans.

INSTRUCTOR: *Oh my God, the rope's breaking!*

(I fall like a giant blancmange onto the rocks below.)

So you can see why I wasn't altogether crazy about going to Pioneer Camp but I just couldn't bring myself to tell Mum and Dad all this. So…

I tried to give the letter to Mum over tea. She was engaged in an argument with Martin at the time. Martin?

Ah, I forgot to tell you. Dad finally got his little football star – four and a half years ago, to be exact. Martin John Mooney – the noisiest four-year-old in the universe. When Martin opens his mouth people on the other side of the estate get perforated eardrums.

Just then Mum was putting a microscopic helping of chicken casserole on his plate.

'Bambi doesn't eat chicken,' he bellowed. 'He only eats grass!'

(At the moment my little brother is being Bambi. He watches the video every single day. He'd watch it ten times a day if Mum let him. He's taken to wearing these red velvet antlers Nanna and Grandpa bought him at Christmas. He even wears them in bed, and Dad has to go up and take them off when he's asleep.)

'Bambi is a deer, and you're a little boy, Martin!'

I could tell Mum was getting exasperated.

'Actually Bambi eats meat sometimes to strengthen his antlers,' I told him.

He gave me a long look.

'It's a well-known fact, son.' Dad put another spoonful on Martin's plate.

'Will my antlers get bigger if I eat all this up?'

'No doubt at all about it,' I said. 'I'll measure them for you after tea if you like.'

I waved the letter at Mum again. 'It's about Pioneer Camp. It's a bit expensive, actually – I don't mind if we can't afford it.' I tried to sound heroic and sad. This was a mistake. Dad's ears shot up.

'Can't afford what, Hazel? If this is something important for your education, of course we can afford it!' Dad whipped the letter out of Mum's hands.

'I thought maybe with you going on short time...' I faltered.

Dad works on the buses, and everyone's had to take a cut in hours – either that or people would have been made redundant.

'Never mind about short time!' Dad was beginning to bluster. 'Your Mum and I have always put a bit away, against bad times. This camp sounds just the job! We want the best for you, Hazel – don't you forget it!'

I thought quickly. Then I had it! On Monday after school I always look after Martin, so Mum can take Nanna shopping.

'But what about Mondays when I mind Martin,' I said, trying to look really concerned.

'No problem, Hazel,' smiled Mum. 'Martin can come with us for once.'

Oh bog it! I could see I was going to have to go to camp, like it or lump it.

'Have my antlers grown yet?'

I felt a pain shoot through my right ear.

'For heaven's sake, Martin,' I protested. 'Can't you talk without shouting?'

'I'm not shouting!' he bellowed. 'I'm just very strong because my antlers have grown!'

I give in.

'Well you'd better whisper for a bit if you want me to measure them – it's a well known fact that shouting makes your antlers shrink!' I could see he was impressed.

We had apple pie for pudding. It seems deer like apple pie.

Dad went straight off after tea to fill in the reply bit of the letter while I measured Bambi's antlers.

Oh well, I thought, at least Leanne will be going too.

Text message:
Lauren Stevenson to Amanda Brierley

F2T? IM :-6 COS OF MOR
DANS PRAC — I H8 IT!
:-) UR GNG 2 CAMP
H U H? DA :@) 'S GNG 2!
NM!
GGN
PAW APU
L

CHAPTER FOUR

My diary - Hazel Mooney

<u>2 October</u>
WIMBLE HALL BOOT CAMP

The worst thing in the world has happened. Am here at Hell Hall - aka Wimble Hall Boot Camp - alone! Well, not alone exactly, since the rest of 9G is here - but with one <u>BIG</u> exception: Leanne!

The day before we left, Leanne's gran was rushed into hospital, and Leanne's whole family dashed off to Cardiff to see her. Leanne was dead upset - about her Gran, AND missing camp. Poor Leanne - I'd hate it if Nanna was really sick.

And it's SO important to have a friend with you when you go away from home. I suppose I couldn't say Leanne is my best friend - I'm just ONE of Leanne's friends, but TO ME she's special. And it's nice to have someone to sit next to on the coach, and things like that. One good thing though - Mum and Dad have bought me a mobile so can call home if I want. Brilliant!

Coach journey not too bad - lots of spare seats, so I had two all to myself. At least no one could grumble about me taking up all the room. Certain people, naming no names (Michael Evans), were really hyper. He stuffed so many crisps the coach had to pull over so he could throw up. He went a horrible yellowish-green, and for a split second I felt sorry for him, even though he is such a dweeb.

Seemed to get here really quickly. When I saw Wimble Hall for the first time, I was

MEGA impressed. It's set in the hills, in Derbyshire. The drive is lined with these enormous trees that make an archway over the road. The leaves had all turned red and amber, and it was like driving through a tunnel of fire. And there's a huge lake in front of the hall, with geese and ducks!

The hall is really old, Tudor or something, with twisty chimneys and little windows with stone archways, all burning gold with the afternoon sun. Was getting really carried away, pretending to be a beautiful Elizabethan girl, coming to stay with my rich cousins...then the coach stopped suddenly and it was back to reality. In your dreams, Hazel!

Then we met the warden, and the instructors. Cool - they're all really young and funky and introduced themselves by their first names!

ANDY: LUSH is the only word! (Cow Features flicking her PERFECT blonde hair at him all the time!)

SHEM: Really, really funny - had us all in tucks straight away!

JULIE: V friendly - said if anyone had any problems or worries to come and see her. I liked her, but can't see me talking about my worries with a stranger.

Then Miss K said four people had to sleep in a log cabin in the grounds because there weren't enough beds in the dorms. Had to be mature and sensible people. (EVERYONE put their hands up, 'cos we'd seen the cabins down by the lake when we arrived - and they looked sooo cute!)

AND GUESS WHO SHE CHOSE!!! Sital, Parvinder, and Jenny and ME!!!!!!!!!!!!!!!!!!!

Hooray! So I'm NOT with CF!
HIP-HIP HOOORAAAAAAY!!!!

We went off to our cabin straight away, and it's super cool - really cosy, with a red, fluffy rug on the floor, and pine bunk beds.

Sital and Parvinder are best buds so they bagged the bunk by the window. Jenny and I just looked at each other.

Jenny's really quiet, and never talks unless you say something to her first. So I asked her if she wanted top or bottom bunk. At first she just shrugs, and says she doesn't mind. But her cheeks glow like red peppers, and what with that and her red hair, she looks like she's going to combust! So I say, OK, shall we toss for it, and she says 'Don't mind' again.

Great - set to be there till midnight, deciding on a bunk bed! Took control, and chose heads; it was tails, so she ummmed and ahhhed and eventually decided on the top bunk. Phhew-weeeee, is all I can say.

*

I'd guessed we'd be in bunk beds, and have had NIGHTMARES imagining the top bunk groaning all night under my weight. What if it collapsed, and I came crashing down on top of her! Could just see the headline in the Leicester Gazette:

PETITE SCHOOLGIRL SMOTHERED BY OVERWEIGHT FRIEND IN COLLAPSED BUNK BED NIGHTMARE!

Aaarrggh! The shame, the horror! I parked myself on the bottom bunk before she could change her mind.

When we were unpacking, I suddenly realised how weird it would be to sleep in the same room as three other people. Truth is, I was worried in case they laughed at my nightshirt - I know everyone wears shortie PJs now, but you have to have really good legs to wear them (like CF). Mum got me this dead cool nightshirt so I wouldn't feel embarrassed. It's dark,

dark blue scattered with silver stars. Mum said it made me look slimmer too.

Had dinner in the Hall in a gigantic dining room - not a bit like school, with long wooden tables, and red tablecloths. Food brill - not school dinner-ish at all. I had roast chicken, with roast pots and veg. There was trifle, ice-cream or fresh fruit afterwards. It was very noisy - especially from Michael Evans's table - but for once no one stopped us, and Shem and Andy and Julie were as noisy as we were!

Sat next to Jenny, and when you get past her shyness, she's really nice. OK - not the same as having Leanne here, but I was beginning to think I might enjoy myself...

(CF too busy fluttering her eyelashes at Andy to talk, and AB really quiet, too. I sometimes wonder why Motormouth chose her as a friend...)

After dinner we had free time. Called Mum and Dad to tell them I'm OK. Felt a bit weepy for a sec, but managed to swallow hard and hide it. Don't want everyone to think I'm a complete wet week!

Mum tried to put Martin on the phone, but he came over all shy, so I blew him a kiss down the phone before I said 'Night-night.' Right at that moment CF walks by with AB! Typical – just my luck!

I heard them snigger, and then CF says, in a silly, baby voice, 'Oh, NIGHTY-NIGHT, Mummy Darling – I miss you so much I want to cry!' Then they both rushed out of the room howling with laughter.

This huge surge of anger went through me like an electric shock.

What IS it with her ? So much for thinking I might enjoy myself – I know, I just know, that COW won't let me.

✱

Suddenly I'd had enough of people, so I went back to the cabin, grabbed this diary, and am now sitting in a quiet, hidden spot where I can write without snidey comments.

The sun's going down and turning the lake to deep crimson and the trees all look like they're lit up from the inside. It's getting chilly, but I don't want to go back yet.

It's weird - only forty miles away there's the city, and all the dirt, and the cars and the petrol fumes. Another world!

1NS UPN A TME THR WUR
3 : @) 5 - MMY : @)
DDY : @) AND HAZEL
: @)
DID U C H'S MA THS A.M.? -
GOTTA SNOUT JST LIK
HAZEL'S !
LMHO
L

CHAPTER FIVE

My diary - Hazel Mooney

<u>3 October</u>
WIMBLE HALL BOOT CAMP - DAY TWO

Today has been really weird. Nearly phoned Mum this morning, but won't 'phone home' every time I feel low. I'll show them I can handle things myself. V glad I bought this diary - almost like having a friend to talk to.

Needn't have worried about my nightshirt last night - Jenny's is pink with teddy bears all over it!!! Came to bed early so I could get undressed without anyone seeing me. And have made v interesting discovery about Jenny Hopkins – she might not talk during the day, but she makes up for it at night!

It was dead cosy in the cabin last night. Sital had this box of juicy dark chocs so we sat around guzzling and giggling till really late – and we all got a bit hyper. Funny what chocolate does to you! Got to know Sital and Parvinder, too – at school they always seem joined at the hip, but they're really cool. As for Jenny – MEGA surprises there!

Later on the wind started whooshing around the cabin and Parvinder kept going on about ghosts and about the hall being haunted! Left the light on for a while, because we all felt so jumpy. S, P and J got off to sleep quite quickly, but I lay awake for ages. Not used to sleeping away from home.

THEN THE <u>FUN</u> STARTED!

Had only been asleep for a few seconds when I heard Jenny talking - LOUDLY! 'It's got great big spots all over it!' she shouted.

'What has?' I said sleepily.

Then there was this MEGA thump overhead, so I got out of bed to have a look. And there was J, flat on her back snoring peacefully! So she talks in her sleep!

AND THAT WAS JUST FOR STARTERS!

She woke me up at least FIVE TIMES in the night, carrying on. Funny thing was, she didn't wake herself up at all. But she did wake P and S up - and then we all got the giggles. Just before dawn our nightlife really hotted up. I was fast asleep, when someone started shaking my arm!

'It's time to change!' Jenny again!
'Change what?' I said all fuddled.
'Move!' commanded Jenny. 'My bed!'

*

She's mad, I thought! Then I saw that although her eyes were wide open they were just staring. She was fast asleep! By now S and P were wide awake.

'What's she DOING?' groaned P.

'My bed!' insisted J. 'Move!'

Nothing for it – I had to move. So I dragged myself out of my bunk and climbed up into the top one. Jenny flopped into my bed, and then silence. AT LAST!

Slept like a log until Julie popped her head round the door at seven o' clock.

'Oh what a night!' I moaned.
'Well, I slept like a top!' said Jenny.

Was truly gobsmacked, but then saw the funny side of it, and nearly ROFL. At this point J twigged! She went bright red.

'Don't worry, Jenny,' I said, 'I haven't laughed so much in ages!'

BUT, if I'd known then what was going to happen later, I'd have got the first train back to Leicester.

Gave Leanne a quick ring straight after breakfast - it was GTT! Leanne's gran much better! So was feeling pretty good when we met up in the big hall to be sorted into teams, even though I'd been worrying about them all last week. The teachers choose them and it's all about learning how to get on together. Much talk about bonding.

Miss K read out the three team lists. In my team (team B) is Sital, (but not Parvinder), Jenny (hurray!), Michael Evans, Dean McCarthy, Lily Chang, Josh Armitage(!!!) and a few others.

And guess who? Yeah - Cow Features. All I

could think was, oh no, not her! I CANNOT bond with her!!!!!

Then Miss K went on about how we'd been put together for a purpose and how we all had to pull together as a team. (Meanwhile CF sniggering to AB - APU.)

Miss K. noticed and gave her the beady eye. 'Do you have something to share with us, Lauren?' she said, in her steely voice.

'Oh no, Miss Kennedy, sorry Miss Kennedy!' said CF, all sugar sweet (yuk!) but I could see she was really peed off.

Our team leader was Andy!!!! and we were going to do abseiling. We went off together into our team room for a little talk.

(On the way heard CF making up to Lily Chang, whispering behind her hands, and giggling. Lily looked dead uncomfortable.

Bet CF's going to get Lily to gang up against me, now she hasn't got AB. Could swear she was looking at me. Went bright red.)

I AM NOT GOING TO LET HER GET TO ME!

Andy explained all about abseiling to us. Tried to listen, but all I could see was that scene where the rope breaks, and there's me splattered on the rocks below.

Andy kept saying we'd be perfectly safe if we followed instructions, and that we didn't have to do anything we really didn't want to, and that as a team we were there to help each other, etc., etc. - and (v important) to have fun. HA HA, I think. OK - so now I knew we didn't HAVE to do something we really didn't fancy, I felt a bit better. But still...

When we got to the abseiling place, there was this GINORMOUS tower that looked like a crazy block of flats - only the walls were made of scaffolding with all this green canvas flapping in the wind. Instead of stairs there were ladders and platforms running right up to the top. Down the whole of one side was this huge slope, the 'rock face' itself! I just stood there and looked up and up.

Then it came to me - I could do it! I felt myself go all hot. Suddenly I wanted to show them all that I'm not a TOTAL nerd!

'Right,' said Andy, 'who's going to be first to the top?'

About five voices shouted 'Me!'

NOT me - I'm not that daft!

Dean McCarthy was waving his hand about like a lunatic, so Andy let him have first go. Andy went up the ladders with Dean. When he got to the top we all cheered like mad.

Then came the really scary part. We all went round to the other side to watch Dean abseil down the wall. He looked so little up there, I felt my heart skip a beat. We saw Andy fixing Dean's harness and adjusting his helmet. Then Dean took hold of the rope and let himself carefully over the edge (aarrgh!). And down and down he came, skimming lightly to the ground.

'That was excellent!' said Dean, all glowing and out of breath.

Then of course everyone wanted a go – even Jenny was begging to try it. Just Sital and I held back. I sort of wanted to, but something was stopping me.

Most people had at least one go, and then the really brave ones started to do clever tricks.

Andy asked if anyone wanted to do a star. Guess who did? CF, of course!

✱

She shot up the ladder with Andy, they had
a quick chat, then she started down the
slope. When she was about halfway down
she suddenly let go of the rope. She
leaned backwards and spread out her
arms and legs against the wall in a star
shape. We all held our breath, and then a
huge cheer went up. OK - have to admit it,
was MEGA impressed. Of course, after that
she was Superstar of Team B. Seemed like
everyone crowded round her, telling her
how brave and brilliant she was... As if she
needs telling!

Then she came past me, smirking. 'Why
don't you have a go, Hazel?' - all sugary
sweet. But I could hear the hidden sneer.

That did it! 'I was just about to, Lauren.'
Strange - I heard my own voice but it didn't
seem to belong to me. Next thing, I was
asking Andy to let me have a go. Sudden
silence. Somewhere, a muffled snigger.

Then Jenny – of all people – shouted, 'Go for it, Hazel!'

I started the climb to the top. At first it wasn't too bad, but then my legs began to ache and tremble, and I found it hard to get my breath. My hands sweated so much they started to slip on the rungs. All the time the wind ripped and roared in the canvas, and I had the feeling that the whole tower was swaying slightly in the wind. Andy kept talking to me, saying I was doing really well, and I was nearly there.

There was this moment when I thought my arms would come out of their sockets, and my leg muscles seemed to be turning to jelly. Then I was there, somehow, on top of the tower, with Andy standing beside me. There was a sudden noise from below, and I realised that the others were CHEERING! And so was Andy.

✳

Then I looked down. A million miles below me was this sea of bobbing heads. The world began to spin, and I grabbed hold of Andy.

'Are you frightened of heights, Hazel?' he said, all calm and gentle.

'I don't know!' I said stupidly. 'I've never been this high up before!'

'Don't worry, Hazel, we'll get you down safely.'

By now the only way I could cope was to close my eyes. Way below me I heard a shriek of laughter. C stinking F! I froze. What a jellyhead I am. A total NERD!

Then I heard another voice beside me, and realised that Miss K was there too. She told me they were going to lower me down the wall because it would be easier than going down the steps. I tried to help, but my muscles had gone so trembly my legs wouldn't work.

✱

Suddenly I felt myself floating, coming
slowly down through the air like a spider on
a thread. I screwed my eyes tight shut. All
I could see in my head was that picture
of the blancmange splattered on the
rocks.

Then I was on the ground with all of Team B
gazing at me with their eyes on stalks. Out
of a mist I saw CF's face swim into focus.
She was enjoying it so much she was
practically wetting herself.

Then the shaking started.

Text message:
Lauren Stevenson to Amanda Brierley

RU F2T?

U SHUDA CN DA : @) 's

FACE WHN SHE CME DWN

DA WALL!

I WAS ROFL!

CU

L

Text message:
Amanda Brierley to Lauren Stevenson

WISH ID BIN THERE!! AND
HAV U CN HER TOP?
GROSS!
G2GN
A

CHAPTER SIX

My diary - Hazel Mooney

<u>4 October</u>

Learned something yesterday - PEOPLE CAN
BE VERY <u>SURPRISING</u>!

There's me, wobbling at the foot of the wall
like a giant lemon jelly, and all around this
weird buzz of voices. Then the voices start
to make sense, and I hear CF sniggering,
and then suddenly - amazingly - I feel
Jenny Hopkins's arm around my shoulders,
and she says, 'Just shut your face, Lauren
Stevenson! Can't you see she's had enough!'

And, even more amazing, CF shut up!!!

*

Andy and Jenny helped me back to the hall - legs still jellified - and then J got me a cup of tea. I began to feel a bit better, but still <u>MEGA</u> embarrassed.

Andy said lots of people are afraid of heights, and it's nothing to be ashamed of, and then Jenny said, 'At least you had the guts to have a go.'

'Everyone will think I'm such a fool,' I muttered. I could still hear Lauren's sniggers.

'Lauren was the only person who laughed, Hazel,' said Jenny. 'And she's such a cow no one takes any notice of her.'

So other people don't like CF! HA!

Went back to the cabin for a bit, then joined the others for lunch. No one said anything about what had happened. Wasn't very hungry, but pretended to eat something. CF and I avoided each other's eyes.

After lunch my team were down for archery. Decided to go along and watch – still felt upset, and legs a bit shaky, but wasn't going to let everyone think I was a total loser, hiding away from them all.

Sat on the grass and watched the others for a bit. Sital was brilliant! Everyone else shooting arrows everywhere BUT the target. Sital must have been Maid Marian in a previous life; she hit the inner ring every time!

'Fantastic!' I shouted.

So Sital tried to get me to have a go. I dithered for a moment, but then said, 'You're on, Sital!'

Andy came across and showed me how to line myself up against the target. (Went hot all over when he steadied my bow arm - hope no one noticed!)

Managed - just about! - to pull the string into position, held my bow steady, and then let the arrow fly.

AND I HIT THE TARGET!!!!!!!!!!!!!!!!

OK, not the inner ring - we can't all be geniuses - but right on the black!

Then my cheeks went on fire, and I nearly cried, because ALMOST EVERYONE WAS CLAPPING AND CHEERING! I know they were only trying to cheer me up after what happened this morning, but it felt really good. And the rest of the afternoon was really cool. Decided I don't care about CF anymore-- not now I've got some real friends - I hope.

And guess what?! CF's a dead loss at archery! She really looked the part - trendy green T-shirt - doing her cool chick bit - but she sent so many arrows flying over the target it was more dangerous than being in Sherwood Forest on a bad day! I did not utter a single giggle when she sent one shooting up into a tree; but it was the BEST MOMENT OF THE DAY!

5 October

Today has been really brilliant too. Had free time a.m. for shopping. Hung out with Jenny and Sital and Parvinder.

Went down to the village - there's all these cute little gift shops, so bought presents to take home. Bought a box of fudge for Dad, a fab scarf for Mum, then saw the perfect present for Martin - a really cute little deer, just like Bambi. (Saw Michael Evans at the sweet counter buying a horrible set of candy false teeth for his poor dad - hope he enjoys them!)

✳

Then we all went into this little cafe for a drink. Parvinder said we ought to try some of the local specialities - so we tucked in. Sital and Parvinder had Bakewell tart and ice cream, Jenny had a chocolate eclair and I had a big frothy mug of hot chocolate with cream on top - not very local but really yummy!

(Saw CF and AB once in the village, but Jenny steered us all into a side street so we didn't bump into them.)

After lunch we were told that our next challenge would involve a lot of team spirit. AAAAARGH!!! More horrible bonding! I knew straight away I'd be faced with CF up front. OK - it's stupid to let one person get to you like that, but I CAN'T HELP IT!!

Julie led us all down to the lake. On the beach were these great stacks of long wooden poles and big blue barrels. There was a heap of strong nylon ropes, a mountain of paddles and a life jacket for each of us. Uh-oh!

Each team had to choose 8 barrels, 10 poles, and some rope. There was a mad scramble while we sorted ourselves out. Julie told us we had to build a raft that would float, take it out onto the lake, paddle round the little island, and back to the landing stage – in a race!

TOTAL CHAOS while we all shouted and argued. Then CF yelled 'Shut up all of you – we'll get nowhere like this!' Sudden silence. 'We need to vote for a leader, otherwise we'll do nothing but argue!'

'Well, I vote for Lauren.' (This from Michael Evans; perhaps he fancies her!)

Suddenly I found my voice. 'And I vote for Sital!' Lauren went bright red with anger.

✳

Josh said we should vote - and only two people voted for CF. Hooray!

Sital took control immediately, and asked who had an idea - one at a time.

'I've got a brilliant idea!' (Michael Evans, of course.) He arranged the barrels in a square, and made a grid like you do for noughts and crosses. Everyone could see what he was trying to do. Within minutes we had the whole raft lashed together. Who'd have thought it - there's obviously more to Michael than meets the eye!

The other teams were still bawling at each other - so we grabbed a paddle each and off we went! AND THE RAFT FLOATED!! Everyone cheered.

But when we climbed onto it there was much frantic waving of arms and legs, then suddenly the raft tipped violently, and

Michael fell right in! More cheering (and hysterical laughter from other two teams).

Michael got out of the water and did a mock bow. 'There will be a repeat performance at seven p.m.!'

Even louder cheers, and I thought, Michael Evans may be as daft as a brush, but he really has got guts.

We all climbed back onto the landing stage. And Sital said we'd have to start again because the raft wasn't stable enough.

Then I had my MEGA-INSPIRATION! 'I know!' I said, feeling a bit silly. 'We need to distribute the weight more equally.'

Startled silence, then CF smiled sweetly. 'You should know a great deal about weight distribution, Hazel.'

COW! COW! I <u>HATE</u> HER, I <u>REALLY</u> DO!

Someone snickered, but Sital came to my rescue. 'Hazel's right,' she said, and she gave CF the beady eye.

So I took Dad's famous advice, and ignored Cow Features. I drew a quick diagram in the mud with my finger, and said we needed to place the barrels in pairs, equally spaced out, with the poles making a big rectangle over them.

'That's it!' shouted Joshua. 'She's got it!'

Another frantic scramble, to remake the raft.

(Meanwhile Team A had made this really cool raft, and were ready to launch.)

But this time our raft floated even with us on it! And now the heat was really on!

✳

(Team C still having a big shouting match - so no worry there!)

Took quite a while to get the hang of the paddles - with everyone going in different directions at first, then Josh appointed himself cox, and we really got going!

(Meanwhile Team A spinning round in slow circles - no cox. Ha!)

There were a few hairy moments when they bashed into us, but after a bit of a water battle, with lots of splashing and shrieking, we finally managed to push ourselves off with our paddles, and head triumphantly towards the little island. Everyone soaked, but MEGA fun.

The sun was sparkling on the lake, and the trees were all aflame with autumn colours. And it was so warm for October! I felt this sudden rush of happiness, like I was lit up inside. We were round the island

and sailing home in triumph before Team C had fully launched their raft!

'Well done, B Team!' yelled Julie.

Suddenly everyone was yelling and cheering. Then – guess what! Josh Armitage comes up to me.

'Brilliant idea that, Hazel!'

Blushed furiously, but felt dead chuffed.

Am now sitting in my hideaway by the lake to write up all of this. What a day! Still feel a bit spaced-out, but deep down I've got this really good feeling inside.

I never knew so many people liked me before.

Suddenly I'm thinking of home. Funny – it's Martin I've been missing most. Thank goodness for my mob. I'll give them all a quick ring now!

Had a quick word with Mum. Martin came on
the phone too. Heard Mum say, 'It's Hazel
on the phone, Martin. Now say "hello" this
time.' Conversation went:

MARTIN: HELLO HAZEL! (Ouch - my ear!)
ME: Hi, Martin - what have you been doing
today? (Long pause.)
ME: Are you there, Martin? (Another long
pause.)
MARTIN: HOW DID YOU GET IN THE PHONE,
HAZEL?
ME: I'm not IN the phone, Martin, I'm a long
way away, talking to you through my mobile.
MARTIN: Oh. (Explanation evidently not gone
down very well.)
MARTIN: Hazel?
ME: Yes, Martin.?
MARTIN: I DON'T LIKE IT WHEN YOU'RE IN THE
PHONE. WILL YOU COME OUT OF IT SOON?
ME: I promise; I'll be home tomorrow - and
I've got a special present for you.
MARTIN: OK... (v doubtfully.)

*

Then I heard Mum tell him to blow me a good-night kiss. Managed to hold my mob a few inches from my ear just in time. Phone must have been RATHER damp in number 3, Burnmoor Crescent!

'Thanks, Marty,' I said. And I blew him a real smacker back.

I'm sitting here, watching the sun turn the whole world to gold. I feel warm and comfortable all over, like something precious is touching me too.

CHAPTER SEVEN

I used to hate Monday mornings. Another week of school, another week of misery, coping with the insults, the sniggers, and the hurtful jokes. But since Pioneer Camp everything has been so much better. OK, before I always had Leanne, but now I could count Jenny, Sital and Parvinder as my friends, too. In a funny way the abseiling disaster was a turning point for me; I could feel that lots of the kids had admired me for at least having a go, and from the moment when everyone cheered in the archery class, I realised that many of them were on my side. Of course, that didn't apply to Cow Features – but suddenly I found I didn't mind about her nearly so much; besides, as Jenny said at camp, not as many people like Lauren as she would like to believe.

The first thing I did when I got back was to

phone Leanne. It was good news. Her gran had improved so much with antibiotics and the care in hospital that she had pulled round and was out of danger. Leanne and I had a lot of catching up to do. I told her about the Great Disaster, how Jenny had stuck up for me, and how everyone had cheered me for having a go.

Then Leanne said, 'Well, I'm not surprised Hazelnut; what you did was really brave – and besides they all *like* you!' And that made me really think.

Anyway, being back at school was a bit of an anticlimax after Wimble Hall, but there was a much friendlier atmosphere in 9G. It was almost Halloween, and a big party was being planned at school, with a disco.

Our year had been decorating our own clothes in Design, and there was talk of a fashion show as well. I love anything artistic, so I decided I would work on a calf-length black halter neck dress for the disco. Leanne came with me, and we found just the right dress on the market, really cheap and plain. Then we hit the girly shops. I chose some glue-on decorations – gorgeous black beads and sequins, with a sort of peacock sheen. Leanne was decorating a denim jacket, and I helped her choose some bits and pieces – a patch pocket, some hearts and ribbons, and a packet of glitter. We stopped at a cafe for a quick bite afterwards. I really enjoy going shopping with Leanne!

So I was looking forward to Design on Monday morning. And Mrs Parsons spotted my dress straightaway. 'Lovely dress, Hazel – wherever did you find it?'

'On the market, Miss.' I could swear I saw Cow Features curl her lips.

Jenny was decorating a plain T-shirt, Sital and Parvinder were practising Mendhi patterns, and Michael Evans and Josh were painting a huge spooky poster to advertise the disco. Leanne was working on her denim jacket.

Mrs Parsons had disappeared into the depths of the needlework cupboard, so we all took the opportunity to relax for a bit. Leanne slipped her now glam jacket on over her school blouse, and struck a model pose, hands on her hips, cheeks sucked in to give her that sultry look. She executed a few mincing steps round our table.

'Whoa, Leanne,' said Leon Josephs, giving her a quick, appreciative wink.

'Stop, stop, it's all too much – my eyes are dazzled!' said Michael Evans, fanning himself and falling backwards over a chair as he pretended to faint. Soon a group of giggling girls had gathered around Leanne. For a moment I felt a twinge of jealousy. I wished I could be like her, so funny and confident.

'If you think my jacket looks good, have a look at Hazel's dress,' said Leanne, waltzing back to our table.

My cheeks burned, and I bent over my work so no one could see it.

'Oh Hazelnut!' said Leanne, in despairing tones.

'That's quite enough noise, 9G,' said Mrs Parsons, staggering out of the cupboard with a huge roll of fabric. 'Settle down now.'

We all snipped and glued companionably until the end of the lesson. By then I was almost done. Mrs Parsons said I could finish my dress off at home.

'Absolutely fabulous, Hazel!' she said, and before I could do anything, she held it up so everyone could see it.

'Oh, Hazel, it's the business!'

It was Cow Features. Her voice was as sweet as honey. There was just the slightest lift of her upper lip as she spoke. But I knew how to deal with her now.

'Thank you, Lauren,' I smiled, but inside I felt my stomach tighten.

She was working on a pair of combat trousers that certainly hadn't come off the market – I can't imagine what they must have cost.

I was packing my bag when I heard it – the quiet pip-pip of my mobile. Whoever could be texting me in class? I bent over my bag so no one could see me and looked at the screen. It read:

WOTS PINK AND BLACK
AND WOBBLES?
A : @) INA MATERNITY
DRESS!

I felt my cheeks flame. A surge of anger and shame went through me.

At the back of the classroom Lauren was demurely packing her own bag. Her lips were twitching ever so slightly. Then the bell went, and everyone bolted for the door.

I felt completely shaken. How had she got my mobile number?

As I hurried home my heart pounded in my ears, and I felt sick. Why was she always on my back? Where had this new torture come from? Perhaps she doesn't like it now I've got more friends. Maybe it's not so easy now to get laughs at my expense and it's making her hate me even more.

But my dress... It had looked so good when Mrs Parsons held it up. Did it really look like a maternity dress?

Then I remembered what Jenny had said about Lauren; 'she's such a cow no one takes any notice of her.' I took a deep breath and strode on homewards, my head held high. By the time I reached the front gate, I had calmed down.

After tea that night Mum helped me put the finishing touches to my dress. We'd had pork chops with roast potatoes and peas, and a feather-light treacle sponge pudding afterwards. There's no doubt our mum is a wonderful cook.

Martin was busy trying to walk up the walls;

he's stopped being Bambi – right now he thinks he's Spiderman. He's got so many bumps and bruises all over him Mum says she's terrified what people will think. Dad was reading the *Leicester Gazette*. It was warm and friendly in the lamplight. The gas fire spluttered and flickered, and cast a soft glow over the room. Suddenly school – Lauren Stevenson and her spiteful tongue – seemed far away, and unimportant. I realised how much my family meant to me.

'That frock looks a treat, Hazel.' Dad was smiling over the top of the paper.

'It's not a frock Dad, it's a dress.' I tried not to laugh. He's so old-fashioned sometimes.

'Hazel!' My left eardrum exploded.

'Yes, Martin?' I sighed.

'Will you make me a Spiderman costume next?'

'I might if you're a good boy – and learn to talk without shouting!'

I got down on my hands and knees and tickled him on his tummy. He can't stand that. Within a minute he was rolling over and over on the floor, giggling hysterically.

'Are you going to stop shouting?' I demanded.

'No!' he squealed, trying to grab my hands.

'Give in!' I said, tickling him on his feet. He *really* can't stand that.

'I give in, I give in!' he bellowed.

I was gasping myself by this time.

'Of course I'll make you a Spiderman costume – if Mum'll help me.'

'You're my bestest friend in all the world!' bawled my little brother, louder than ever – if that's possible!

Honestly, sometimes you just can't win!

CHAPTER EIGHT

'Why couldn't the skeleton go to the disco?'

A chorus of groans greeted Michael Evans's latest awful joke. It was Monday 31ˢᵗ October, and 9G were in Design, putting the finishing touches to the Halloween preparations.

I took pity on Michael 'Go on, then, why couldn't the skeleton go to the disco?' I said shyly.

'Because he had no body to go with!' shouted Michael triumphantly.

There were even louder groans, and Leon hit him over the head with a balloon.

We were having fun though.

The Design area is a brand new block in the school, and opens up into lots of interconnecting rooms. You could do Pottery, or Metalwork, Art, Technology, Fashion – lots of things. There was going to be a fashion show early in the evening, and then a fancy-dress disco afterwards. Some kids were working on their costumes, and others were in charge of spooky decorations. Josh was in the hall with Sital constructing an enormous spider's web from silver cord. I was adding a few last-minute touches to my dress, when a tall Year Eleven lad stuck his head round the door.

'Is Hazel Mooney in here?' he called.

'Yes,' I answered, startled.

'Mr Simmonds wants to see you in his office now!'

Oh sugar – what had I done? All of 9G were staring, goggle-eyed.

'You'd better go straight away, Hazel,' said Mrs Parsons.

I'm not the sort of girl who's usually in trouble. I hurried down the corridor to Mr Simmonds's room, my cheeks burning.

'Come!' shouted a deep voice, when I knocked nervously on the door.

To my enormous relief Mr Simmonds was smiling.

'Ah – sit down a minute, Hazel.' He busied himself with some papers on his desk for a few moments. 'Now, Hazel, you're probably wondering why I sent for you?'

I nodded speechlessly.

'Your form tutor, Miss Kennedy, and I have been watching you very closely, lately.'

Hell's bells, it must be something awful!

'And I have to tell you that we are very pleased with your progress!'

My eyebrows shot up so much Mr Simmonds laughed.

'We were very impressed with the courage you showed in Pioneer Camp, and I have a glowing report from Mrs Jessop of the effort you have been putting into your Maths lately.'

It was true that I'd been doing much better in Maths since the camp. Perhaps my success as a raft-builder had spilled over into other problem solving!

'In fact, if it continues, I'm sure we'll be moving you up to set two in the New Year. I also hear you have been making a fabulous dress in Design!'

My cheeks flamed. I couldn't think of anything to say, so I nodded again.

'Unfortunately, one of the girls has had to pull out of the fashion show tonight. So, I would like you to consider modelling your dress in her place, Hazel. No,' – seeing the look on my face – 'don't give me an answer now, just think it over.'

I walked out of Mr Simmonds's office with my head in a whirl. Set two for Maths – that was quite something. But the fashion show: that was another matter. I imagined myself walking down the catwalk. I heard Lauren's voice say, 'What's pink and black, and wobbles?'

No! I just couldn't do it. Then I heard Mr Simmonds's voice in my head. 'We were very impressed with your courage.'

Suddenly I stood up tall, and thought about this new version of myself. I heard an echo in my head – Jenny Hopkins's voice this time shouting, 'Go for it, Hazel!'

That did it. I made up my mind to take part in the Fashion Show that night, just as I reached the Design room.

I opened the door and walked in. Then I froze.

The classroom was in uproar. Mrs Parsons was nowhere to be seen. Lauren Stevenson was mincing up and down on an improvised catwalk made from a row of tables.

And she was wearing my dress.

She had stuffed two balloons into the bodice, and an enormous one over her stomach. She strode out with an exaggerated, slinky walk.

'Hello fans, I'm Hazel Pig: don't you just love my sexy new maternity dress?' she purred.

What happened next I can only remember in a haze, as if it's a nightmare sequence.

I heard Leanne – *Leanne* – give a snort of laughter, and I saw myself running like a lunatic towards Lauren. I remember grabbing hold of the hem of my dress and pulling it violently. I saw Lauren half falling from the desk, as I tugged it over her head. Balloons popped and exploded. Lauren gave a scream as the zip caught in her hair for a moment.

I dimly remember grabbing my bag, and then I was running – out of the classroom, out of the school drive – and home at last along Spice Lane.

CHAPTER NINE

My diary - Hazel Mooney

<u>2 November</u>

I HATE MYSELF.

Hate my <u>STUPID</u> **BIG** **FAT** <u>UGLY</u> body.
Hate everyone at school, especially Lauren
Stevenson, Cow Features. And I hate this
garage. It's freezing cold, and crawling
with spiders. The wind blows in through a
gap under the door, and the windows are
running with condensation. Light doesn't
work, either.

Haven't been to school since Monday, and
I'm NEVER going back again. Can't even

write about it without feeling sick, and crying all over again. Stuffed that gross, disgusting maternity dress down the back of my wardrobe. There were great tufts of CF's hair caught in the zip.

I hope it <u>REALLY</u> <u>HURT</u> <u>HER</u>.

Can't believe I was even considering modelling it for the fashion show. I will <u>NEVER</u>, <u>EVER</u> look at it again. Have finally REALLY seen myself as other people do - a great big ridiculous <u>FAT</u> <u>LUMP</u>.

Can't stop seeing it all in my head - CF strutting up and down, huge, swollen and grotesque, in my dress. But what hurts me most - Leanne was laughing too. Laughing AT me. I won't ever forget that, or forgive her. I really thought she was my friend. I'm obviously so GROSS, and FAT that no one likes me. Not even Leanne.

Have never felt so alone in my life. Hazel No-mates, that's me.

Did NOT go to Halloween Disco. Mum and Dad went on and on, so pretended I was ill, and went to bed early. Then lay in the dark, and cried.

Leanne called my mob a few times, but I ignored it. Then she rang on the phone downstairs, but I got Mum to tell her I was sick. Don't think Leanne gave me away, though - Mum didn't say anything about it.

Hid in the garage yesterday during school. Got dressed in my school uniform as usual, headed off towards school, then when I was sure Mum had taken Martin to Nanna's and gone off to work, sneaked back home. Can't get in the house because I've lost my key - again - and Mum and Dad have refused to get another one cut since it's the third one I've lost.

So here I am, stuck in the garage. Am so cold, may never be warm again.

*

Got my school books in my bag, but don't feel like reading them, so earlier went round to the paper shop and bought a magazine.

Been reading the problem page: I WAS DUMPED FOR THE CLASS TART; MY BOYF CHEATS ON ME; MY BEST FRIEND STOLE MY MAN!

Big deal - at least they've had boyfriends. Who's gonna go out with a lump of lard? There was this girl who thought she was hideous because of her acne; can understand that more, but I'd swap any day! Buy a stick of spot-concealer, and you're fixed aren't you?! No such thing as a fat-concealer.

Have just bought myself a king-sized chocolate bar, and a can of cola. Why not - got nothing to lose.

Mob keeps ringing and bleeping - mostly

Leanne, though Jenny rang once. NO WAY am I answering! Have deleted messages without reading them. Am too angry.

Something horrible has just happened. I got a text message from CF. Knew I shouldn't look, but couldn't stop myself. It said:

HI : @) SO WHR R U HIDING?
YOYO NOW. JUST U W8 - U CAN'T ESCAPE ME.

My stomach's all knotted and my mouth's full of saliva.

Can't stop shaking.

What am I going to do?

CAN" tell Mum and Dad - would have to tell them EVERYTHING - the dress, the bullying... I'm so ashamed.

I just can't do it.

WEDNESDAY EVENING

It's happened again. There's been another message. Just couldn't stop myself looking. It said:

HI : @)
WOT STILL ALIVE?

I feel cold all over, I'm shaking again.

I am so afraid.

Why does she hate me so much? What have I ever done to her?

I'm NEVER, ever, EVER going back to that school. I'll forge a letter to Miss Kennedy. Don't care if I shouldn't. I'll say I'm ill, and won't be in all week. Natural-born liar, me. Mum's handwriting v easy to copy, so's her signature. Don't know what I'll do next week, but I'll think of something. Have to.

✳

3 November

This morning bribed Michael Evans's sister, in Year Seven, to take the letter to school for me. She promised not to tell. They live just round the corner from us, but Michael wouldn't be seen dead walking to school with his sister, so I was safe.

Think Mum and Dad suspect something – they keep asking me if I'm OK. Told them I've got a bit of a cold. Which I have.

Have to sneak out of the garage every day before Mum gets back with Martin in the early afternoon, so I can pretend to come home from school at usual time. End up walking round the streets. It's not a lot of fun on Spice Lane Estate on a foggy day in November. I'm catching every kind of cold going.

Great fun. Not.

Today, went to the launderette. It's lovely and warm sitting watching the washing going round and round. Till I realised what a loser I must look like.

No, cross that out – what a loser I AM.

Then it happened again: I got another message from CF. I knew it was stupid to look. Knew I shouldn't. But I did. It said:

DIE : @) DIE

The floor waved up and down, and for a moment I went black.

When I came round, there was this old lady in a pink tracksuit bending over me, asking me if I was all right. Think I must have fainted. Managed to get on my feet, and stumbled outside. Could hardly walk though – legs so shaky.

Does Lauren really hate me so much that she wants me DEAD?

Why? Why me?

Spent the afternoon wandering the streets. Huge relief when three-thirty came and I could go back home. Can't face another day like this and can't face school again, ever.

4 November

Four days I've been sitting in this hole. My eyes hurt from crying. My hands are so blue I can hardly hold the pen. Hope I catch double pneumonia. Then they really will have to keep me off school for a long time.

Been having really bad thoughts today. Know now what people mean when they say 'I wish I was dead.'

✳

I'm so fat and ugly I don't deserve to live.
I don't think I'll do anything stupid - I
couldn't hurt Martin or Mum and Dad like
that, and I'm too much of a coward
anyway. But I can't see any way out of
this mess.

What am I going to do? Can't hide here
for ever, and can't go back to that school.
I can't, I really can't...

Keep seeing it all over and over, Lauren on
the catwalk, in my dress, and everyone
screaming with laughter.

I don't know what to do.

I can't breathe...

FRIDAY EVENING

How much can change in a few hours! I'm
sitting in the living room, tucked up on the

sofa, between Mum and Dad, writing this...
My mind keeps slipping back to those last,
dark moments alone in the garage.

There I am, sitting on the garden chair,
frozen, panicking, struggling for breath. I
can't stop crying.

Then outside a car draws up, a door slams,
and I hear footsteps. The garage door
swings open, and there is Dad. His eyes
are wide with astonishment. I run towards
him, and then his big strong arms are
round me, and I am crying like a three-
year-old.

CHAPTER TEN

3, Burnmoor Crescent,
Spice Lane,
Leicester
LE1 6PJ

4th November

Dear Mr Edwards,

We are writing this letter to say that we urgently need to talk to you about our daughter Hazel Mooney. Things have been going on at the school that we are very unhappy about, and we shall not be allowing Hazel to return to school until we are sure these problems have been sorted out. We would like to arrange to see you as soon as possible, since this is an urgent matter.

Yours sincerely,

D. J. Mooney

K. Mooney

This is the letter Mum and Dad wrote to the head. I can't get over how great they have both been. I thought I was really going to get into big trouble for what I've done this week. When I'd finished crying all over him, I told Dad everything – about how I used to get teased all the time for being so fat, about Lauren, about how I thought Pioneer Camp had changed everything, and about what happened at school on Halloween. I told him the whole truth – about the forged letter and the week hiding in the garage too.

And I told him about the text messages.

But he wasn't a bit angry with me! He just put his arm around my shoulders and said, 'Well, thank God I came home early from work today! As for not going to school, and forging that letter – that was wrong, Hazel – you know that. But, well…we knew you were teased sometimes – about being a bit overweight – but we had no idea how serious it had become. Why ever didn't you tell us what's been going on?'

I tried to tell him how ashamed I was, how I didn't want them to know how bad it had got at school and how weak I felt for not being able to deal with it on my own. It's hard to explain, but you want your parents to think people like you – almost as if you have to protect them from the truth.

'The worst thing was the text messages – and seeing Leanne laughing with all the others.' My voice shook when I said this. I still couldn't cope with that memory.

'I shall have a lot to say to your headmaster about those messages, Hazel,' said Dad quietly. 'But none of this is your fault, you know. You shouldn't feel ashamed. And don't forget, Leanne's tried to contact you several times this week; maybe she's got something she wants to say to you.'

I wiped the tears from my nose with my hand. Dad gave me his handkerchief.

After tea, when Martin had been put to bed, Dad sat Mum down and told her all about it.

'I'd like to get my hands on that Lauren Stevenson!' said Mum wrathfully.

But Dad said that wouldn't solve anything, and that he was going to write a letter to Mr Edwards. And he said I didn't have to go back until it had all been sorted out. And that if the school didn't sort it out, he and Mum would find me a new school.

Oh no, I thought, now it will all come out. Now everyone will know all about it. I can just imagine all the gossip in the playground:

'Guess what – Hazel Mooney's parents came into school today…'

'Did you hear what Lauren Stevenson did with Hazel Mooney's dress…'

'Hey – guess what she called her…'

And so on.

And not just the kids – all the teachers would be talking about it too.

It's so humiliating!

I felt really torn in two; on the one hand I knew I needed help, and that the bullying had to stop. On the other hand it would be so horrible to go back to the same school, to have everyone staring at me, probably pitying me too.

Perhaps it would be better to go to another school. But then, the bullying might start all over again, and besides, I had just begun to make friends...or at least, I thought I had.

In the end we agreed that Mum and Dad *should* write to Mr Edwards. They showed me the letter when they'd finished it. Mum wrote it she's good at English like me. Dad gets all tied up when he writes letters.

Then Dad stuck a first-class stamp on it, and posted it. I knew it would reach school on Monday morning, and I felt glad they weren't going to make me go back straight away. But in a funny way, I felt enormously relieved that the letter had been sent. The past week had been hell, and knowing my parents were so completely on my side gave me a nice warm feeling. Why ever hadn't I talked to them before?

Later that evening, Mum fetched my dress from the back of the wardrobe. I still didn't ever want to see it again, but Mum talked me into looking it over. The damage to the zip wasn't as bad as I thought it would be. Mum said it could easily be repaired. She did a brilliant job, but I don't think I'll ever want to wear it.

Saturday was Bonfire Night. Usually I love 5th November, but I couldn't work up any enthusiasm this year. Martin was all excited about it though, so I went to the newspaper shop with Mum. We bought some volcanoes and Roman candles and some sparklers. The Boy With the GOLDEN Voice doesn't like bangers!

Mum put some jacket potatoes and sausages in the oven and we prepared to have a quiet family celebration in the back garden. Just as it was getting dark, and the first rockets were making rainbows in the night, there was a knock at the front door. Mum was busy turning the sausages, so I went to open it.

It was Leanne.

For a split second I nearly closed the door in her face, and then before I could say anything she looked me straight in the eyes, and said, 'I've come to say I'm really sorry for laughing, Hazel, and I've brought a letter from all of us.' She shoved the letter in my hand.

I just stood there looking stupid, and

then suddenly I felt tears prickling the back of my nose.

'Don't stand out there in the dark, you great banana,' I sniffed. 'Come on in!'

CHAPTER ELEVEN

Dear Hazel,

This letter is to say we are all very sorry for laughing when Lauren was pratting about in your dress. We were not really laughing at *you*, and we think your dress is very nice. We are sorry you are poorly, and we hope you will soon be back at school.

Your friends,

Leanne   Jenny

Sean   Parrinder   Michael   Jean

Josh   Lily   Leon

Andrew

Leanne stayed at our house on Bonfire Night. I'd really hated falling out with her, and I felt so much better when I'd read the letter. Maybe they don't hate me after all. Though I noticed that Cow Features's signature wasn't there, or Amanda Brierley's. We went up to my room so we could have a good chat in private. I told Leanne everything that had happened; the week hiding in the garage – the cold, the loneliness, the despair. And above all, the text messaging.

Leanne was horrified. 'That 's so *evil*, Hazel. I mean, I know she's always been a bitch, but to do that...'

Then we talked about what had happened after I ran out of school.

'It was a real madhouse, Hazelnut,' said Leanne, giving me an affectionate thump. 'Total chaos – tables upside down, everyone shouting, and Lauren howling on the floor clutching her head. Mind you, no one took any notice of her except Amanda Brierley. She was making a right fuss over Lauren. "Oh no, you're *bleeding*!"' she mimicked.

'Ha,' I said.

'I ran after you, you know, but you shot off at

such speed I couldn't find you anywhere. I looked up on the bank, behind the mobiles, in the girls' toilets – all over. Then Mr Simmonds spotted me, and I had to go back to class.'

'What did Mrs Parsons say?'

'Oh – she never found out! By the time she got back to the Design room, we'd put everything straight. No one said anything, because we all thought we'd get done. I *did* think of telling Miss Kennedy about it, but I thought I might get *you* into trouble, if they knew you'd run out of school. So I said you'd felt sick really suddenly, and gone home. Still, it would have been better if it hadn't…'

Suddenly Leanne gave me a big hug. I felt tears pricking the back of my nose. I felt warm all over, and inside, something began to heal.

I didn't go back to school on Monday, but Mum and Dad had a phone call from Mr Edwards, asking us all to go in first thing on Tuesday morning. He and Dad had a long chat, and Dad told him everything. Leanne phoned after school and said everyone had had to go and see Mr Simmonds and they'd all got really done, but not to worry – no one was cross with me.

Lauren spent half an hour on her own with Mr Simmonds and the head.

I felt a bit guilty about the others getting into trouble – *they* weren't being horrible really, just insensitive.

On Tuesday morning, I woke up with a feeling of dread like a heavy stone in my stomach. It was going to be hard to face everyone again. Mum and Dad got all dressed up to go to school. I told them there was no need, but they insisted. Dad even put his suit on, and he hasn't worn that since Aunty Anne's wedding!

We had an appointment for nine-thirty, so I didn't have to face everyone straight away, thank goodness. We went to Mr Edwards's office. At first I thought he was going to be really angry with me about the forged letter. It wasn't so much that I minded him telling me off – more that I didn't want him to be disappointed in me.

'We know what Hazel did was wrong, Mr Edwards,' said Dad quietly, 'and she is in no doubt that we disapprove very much of sending a forged letter, and staying off school without permission, but we both feel very distressed about what she has been going through lately.'

Mr Edwards nodded. 'And we share your concern, Mr Mooney. Hazel has been – unbeknown to us – the subject of serious bullying. Hazel's form teacher had alerted us to some of the teasing she was facing, but we had no idea of the true nature of the bullying. And we want to assure you that we do not tolerate bullying at Alderman Newbold's, we are proud of our anti-bullying policy. But what has happened to Hazel has made us aware of some inadequacies in our handling of the situation in Year Nine. Consequently we have taken the very serious step of suspending the ringleader in the affair for one week. And I also want to assure you that if things don't improve, we will consider expulsion. We shall be seeing her parents tomorrow.'

Oh good grief, I thought, she'll hate me worse than ever now!

Mum was nodding approvingly.

'Well, I think you've done the right thing,' she said. 'I find it very upsetting, Mr Edwards, to think of Hazel so frightened of school that she locks herself away in a dark, cold garage for a week. And those text messages were vile, really vile. She might – well, there's no telling what she might have been driven to.'

I squirmed, and wished Mum wouldn't go on.

'Now, Hazel,I want you to promise me that if there is more bullying *of any sort whatsoever*, you will let Miss Kennedy or Mr Simmonds know immediately.' Mr Edwards looked me straight in the eyes.

I nodded.

'And I shall be asking for your help in coming up with a new plan to fight bullying. I'll talk to you about that later. Meanwhile, Leanne is waiting for you outside the door. You're just in time for period two.'

I blushed furiously, and went outside. Mr Edwards continued to talk to Mum and Dad. Outside Leanne was propping up the office wall.

'You've made it just in time for Maths Hazelnut!' She pulled a face, and I laughed in spite of myself. Then she linked arms with me and we walked down the corridor together.

E-mail:
Lauren Stevenson to Amanda Brierley.

Can't phone – Dad's confiscated my mobile.

Can't come out, can't EVER come out again – I've been grounded for a month.

SHIT SHIT SHIT.

I hate my Dad. He's been so horrible, Manda. And all because of that shitty pig.

The only good news is that they've said I can't go in for the dance competition. As if I care – I didn't want to do the bloody thing anyway. And they keep going on about the shame I've brought on the family. AND my dad's asked for extra homework, and they keep CHECKING all the time to see if I'm working. They think I'm doing homework now.

I hate that fat pig. And I hate both my parents. They'll be sorry one day.
L

CHAPTER TWELVE

That first day back was not as bad as I thought it would be. For one thing, I only had to meet about four people from my form in Maths, because we're all split up into different sets. Leanne stuck to me like glue all day – and I was really glad of that. It helped when I met all the others in form period after lunch. Miss Kennedy was dead nice, and didn't draw attention to me at all – just gave me a really warm smile, and left us all to chat.

Everyone seemed glad to see me back. I had a horrible feeling they'd been told to be nice to me, but after a bit we all relaxed and started talking normally and well, it felt good. It was a great relief to me that Lauren wasn't there. No one mentioned her.

Mum and Dad must have had a long chat that day, before I got home, because Mum said she had something she wanted to talk to me about after tea.

'Your Dad and I both feel that we are partly to blame for what's been going on, Hazel,' she said quietly.

'How can you be to blame?' I asked, puzzled.

'We should never have let you get overweight in the first place, Hazel. And it's not just you. Look at us – with the exception of Martin we're all a lot heavier than we should be!'

'But that's the way we are in our family! You, Dad, me, Nanna – we're all big people!'

Dad smiled. 'But we could all benefit from losing a bit of weight. We thought we could try seeing the dietician at the Health Centre, to help us all get fitter. We love you the way you are, Hazel, but it's not good for your health for you to be overweight – and I know I'd feel a lot better if I lost a couple of stones.'

I felt bewildered by this turn of affairs.

'But we're not fat because we eat too much, Dad – it's in our genes! You and Mum have always said so!'

'I know, love,' said Mum. 'We know we're not greedy people, but something must be wrong somewhere, so I think we should all try to get a bit of help. I mean – no one wants to be a stick insect, for heaven's sake – but I think we could all be a bit healthier if we tried.'

All in all, it was a very surprising week. I agreed to go to see the dietician with Mum and Dad. She weighed us all and sent us home with food diaries to fill in.

I'm not telling anyone what I weigh, but it's more than I thought it was.

We had to write down every single thing we ate and drank over the week, and return with the completed diaries in seven days time. It seemed a bit silly to me, but I agreed to do it.

Meanwhile lots of other things were happening at school. All our year were given a talk on bullying, and shown a film. It really made me think. I'd no idea there were so many different kinds of bullying. People usually think it means big kids hitting little kids, but it's much more complicated than that – and don't I know it! OK, bullying can be physical, but words can be just as cruel as blows. As for me, I've been so wrapped up in my own miseries, I hadn't noticed all the other kids who'd been victims of bullying.

We had a discussion afterwards, where we could talk about anything that was worrying us. It was a real eye-opener. Michael Evans said he hated being teased because he was so small for his age. I thought it was really brave of him to say that. No one laughed at him, because we knew what a hard thing it was to admit.

Parvinder said she was sick of racist insults, like 'Paki' and remarks like 'Why don't you go home to your own country?' 'I was born here, like the rest of you,' she said. 'And it really hurts.'

Leanne nodded, and said she'd had to put up with the same sort of thing.

Then Jenny said that when she was in Year Seven some older girls had made her pay 'protection' money to them – they'd called it 'taxing' – and had threatened to beat her up if she didn't. I was really shocked. (Perhaps that's why Jenny has always been so quiet, tiptoeing around almost as if she's afraid.) So I was not alone! I must have been going around with my eyes shut.

Afterwards Mr Simmonds asked us if we had any ideas how we could stop bullying.

'The worst thing about being bullied is being afraid to tell anyone about it,' said Jenny. 'You're afraid that if you tell, you'll be called a snitch, and everyone will think you're a baby. Plus, the bullying will get worse!'

I stared in amazement at Jenny; I wasn't the only person who'd changed since Pioneer Camp!

'And you feel so ashamed,' I added. 'I didn't even want to tell my parents!'

'Well, perhaps that's the first thing we should change,' said Miss Kennedy. 'Bullies rely on you being too scared of ridicule or violence to "tell". But it's vitally important that you should tell someone straight away. A teacher, or a parent.'

'Miss, I've got a good idea,' said Parvinder shyly. 'It would be much easier to tell someone of around your own age than a teacher, or your Mum and Dad. Why don't we have a group of kids that others can go to if they're being bullied?'

'Now that's a brilliant idea,' said Miss Kennedy.

So that was how the school Mediation Service started. Ten kids were to be chosen from each year and specially trained as mediators. The idea was that when someone needed to talk about being bullied they could go to a mediator for help. Usually the mediators would work in pairs, and try to get both the bully and the victim together, to resolve the problem. There were really strict rules on what they could and couldn't do, and if things were really bad, they could call in a member of staff.

There was a special assembly about the scheme, and two trained mediators – Jamal and Kerry – came to school to show us how mediation works. They were brilliant, and made us all laugh!

We were told that anyone could apply to be trained as a mediator. Leanne talked me into applying; I said *I* would, if *she* would, so we both applied. We had to get these forms filled in by other kids, to say why they thought we'd make good mediators – dead embarrassing! Finally, ten kids were chosen from each year.

Now for the amazing part. I was chosen to be a mediator! So were Leanne, Parvinder, Jenny and Michael Evans.

Mr Simmonds said he thought Jenny and I would really understand about bullying from the inside. We were given special training sessions, showing us what to look out for, how to resolve conflicts, and how to handle other people's confidences. I felt dead proud.

And there was another thing; it was funny, but

seeing how many other people had been bullied, how *they* had felt alone and afraid just like me, had made me feel more confident. I was not so odd after all. I felt a huge weight lift from me.

And talking of weight, Mum, Dad and I went back to the dietician with our food diaries. She spent some time looking at them in silence, and then she smiled at us all.

'Well, the first thing to say is something very positive. You're basically eating a good diet – no junk food, and lots of healthy fresh fruit and vegetables!'

We all felt relieved – especially poor Mum; she felt as if she was on trial.

'But – the fat and sugar content of your diet is much too high, especially for nowadays. Our great-grandparents got away with treacle sponge – think of all the carpet beating, and hand washing they did daily. But we don't need to be so active any more, so we're often not! I'm going to give you a diet sheet that will enable you to eat many of the foods you like, but using healthier fats, and replacing things like white bread with wholemeal. And don't worry; it won't all be rabbit food,' she said, seeing the look on Dad's face! 'There's lots of delicious puds you can have if you want them – and you won't ever go hungry, either!'

Mum had gone very red, but she was nodding energetically. 'I'll do anything to help Hazel!'

'And it'll do the rest of us good as well!' said Dad manfully.

I linked arms with them both as we walked home along Spice Lane.

CHAPTER THIRTEEN

It's a week since we went to see the dietician with our diaries. First thing on Monday morning, before school, we all went up to the Health Centre to be weighed again. I've been really good, sticking to the diet. Actually it wasn't all that hard because Mum took what the dietician had said very seriously, and spent hours making all these delicious healthy meals. And I was allowed a treat every day as well, like a mini chocolate bar, plus as much in the way of fruit and vegetables as I wanted to eat. We had all lost weight, but I had lost the most – three pounds!

I was on a high all day. My school skirt feels loose around the waist already, and I keep thinking about all the lovely new clothes I'll be able to wear when I'm a bit slimmer.

I've been making an effort to do more exercise

as well and I've had plenty of opportunities right here at home; Dad's enrolled Martin in the Leicester Lioncubs under fives! So Dad's little football star (at last!) trots off every Saturday morning for his training session in his Manchester United kit, proper little footie boots and all. Dad stays and watches; he says it's hilarious – most of the time they're all running in the wrong direction!

And naturally, a future Beckham needs to practise at home, so guess who ends up in goal...

SCENE: The back garden, 3, Burnmoor Crescent – Sunday morning
(I stand in goal, which at present is the washing basket and a cardboard box. Martin doesn't know this, but Mum and Dad are saving up to buy him a proper goal for Christmas.)

MARTIN: And Beckham comes down the field...yes, he's got the ball...and he shoots! Oh what a shot! (The ball goes a good metre wide of the goal.)

MARTIN: GOAL!

ME: *Martin, you were well out there!*

MARTIN: *(Ignoring me.) ...and now it's a penalty...and yes, Beckham does it again!*

(I throw myself at the ball, and by some miracle stop it.)

MARTIN: *(Ignoring me again.) GOAL!*

And so it went on all morning. One especially brilliant shot went up into the apple tree, so I got plenty of really good exercise, and a scraped knee, getting it down!

And I've been doing something that is just for me. I'm not really a sporty person, to be honest, but I do like swimming, and I made up my mind to go. I felt nervous about being seen in public in a bathing costume, but Leanne said she'd come with me. We went to Raylestone Leisure Centre on Sunday afternoon. When I go with Mum and Dad and Martin, I always have my own cubicle, but Leanne went straight into the big family changing room.

Oh God, I thought, everyone will stare at me when I get changed. But I managed to wrap myself in a towel, and get ready in some privacy. Leanne looks so trim in her costume that I felt really uncomfortable as we splashed through the footbath together.

'I like your new cozzie, Hazelnut,' said Leanne. 'You can really see you've lost weight.'

Good old Leanne! Whatever would I do without her?

Still, I was relieved once I was hidden by the water.

I love swimming – at least that's something you can be good at if you're fat. We fooled about for ages, and had a dead brilliant time. Then I decided I wanted to see how many lengths I could do, so Leanne went off to do some diving in the deep end. I swam ten lengths, and felt really pleased with myself. I rested on the bar for a moment and watched Leanne dive. That's something I'm not so good at but Leanne cuts through the water like a dolphin.

'Race you to the side!' I shouted, and we both shot off across the pool. Leanne won, of course, but we were both giggling and spluttering when we reached the edge.

'I think I've drunk half the pool!' I gasped.

I'd forgotten how much I like swimming, and made up my mind to go once a week.

When I got back from school on Monday Mum met me at the door. She looked rather flustered.

'I've just had a phone call from Mrs Stevenson, Hazel.'

Mrs Stevenson? The name didn't click into place for a moment. Then light dawned.

'Cow Features's mother! Whatever did she want?'

'Hazel!' Mum clicked her tongue reprovingly. 'The thing is, Lauren is returning to school in the morning, and her parents want to bring her round here beforehand so that she can apologise to you.'

Lauren Stevenson at our house! It was too terrible to think about.

'You haven't said yes, Mum?' I could read the answer in her face.

'Well, Hazel, if Lauren wants to apologise to you, I think that's a good thing. After all, you are going to have to get on together, being in the same form and everything. And her mother sounded a really nice person.'

'But she hates me, Mum! She'll only be doing it because she's been made to!'

Mum's face took on a funny set expression that I knew well. 'I'm sorry Hazel, but I think it's for the best. You can't go on being enemies for ever. Far better to make it up now than leave it till school in the morning.'

'When are they coming?' I asked glumly

'At four o' clock, love.'

I looked at the clock. It said three forty-five.

'Oh Mum!' I groaned.

I went in the front room and fumed silently. Martin was watching *Spiderman* and rolling around the floor throwing invisible webs over his toys.

I noticed suddenly how shabby the sofa looks. And the carpet has marks all over it, too.

I did not want her in our house, turning her nose up at everything.

Mum never thinks about things like that. But the Stevensons live in Pebblegate, on the other side of Spice Lane. It's all big detached houses and posh cars. I bet they've never been in a council house before!

I suddenly found I was chewing my fingernails viciously.

I started as I heard a car pull up outside. It was a big Mercedes four by four – this year's model.

Oh no! *Both* of her parents had come. I could just make out Lauren in the back. She looked as sick as I felt.

Mrs Stevenson led the way down the garden path, followed by Lauren with her father close on her heels. She looked like a prisoner.

I heard Mum open the front door, and show them into the back room. Then she called, 'Hazel!'

Oh well, better get it over with, I thought.

Lauren's parents were both very tall and posh. Mrs Stevenson was wearing a smart black trouser suit, with elegant kitten heels. It was like looking at Lauren's double – or perhaps an older sister. There was Lauren's smooth blonde hair, the perfect features, the long slim legs. She didn't look a day older than thirty.

Her Dad was all Italian designer from head to toe – silk tie from Savile Row, expensive shoes, the lot. His eyes flicked rapidly around our living room, lit briefly on Mum and me, and took in the carpet and the stains on the sofa. Such cold eyes. There was something reptilian about Mr Stevenson.

Mrs Stevenson was cracking her lips into a frosty smile. 'Lauren has something to say to you, Hazel.'

Lauren was staring at the carpet. Her father poked her sharply in the back.

'I'm very sorry I was so unkind to you, Hazel,' she recited, 'and I won't do it again.'

Our eyes did not meet. Lauren was gazing at a fixed spot on the carpet as if her life depended on it.

'That's all right,' I muttered awkwardly.

There was a horrible silence, broken by Martin. I've never been so pleased to hear his voice.

'Are we having tea soon, Mum?' he bellowed. 'I'm starving!'

The parents all laughed nervously.

'In a little while,' answered Mum self-consciously. Then she said it. 'Would Lauren like to stay for tea, Mrs Stevenson? She'd be very welcome.'

I saw the look of total horror on Lauren's face. It must have been a mirror image of mine.

Why do parents do these awful things?

'That's very kind of you, Mrs Mooney,'

said Lauren's father. 'I'm sure Lauren would be delighted.'

You could see the look of relief on his face. He simply couldn't wait to get out of the door. So that was that. There were a few polite noises, and they were gone. Suddenly Lauren and I found ourselves alone in the room.

'Look,' I said, 'I'm sorry your parents made you do all this.'

For the first time Lauren's eyes met mine. Her face was white, and her eyes full of angry tears. I looked away.

'Now, Hazel.' Mum bustled in from the kitchen, trying to sound bright and positive. 'Why don't you take Lauren up to your room for a bit while I get tea?'

Oh gross! Mum really meant it! As if I was going to let *her* loose in my room! I could just imagine her at school, passing round all the juicy details of Hazel's little pig-pen. No way!

Then I thought, OK, I've got to do something with her; how about a walk? Not ideal, a walk around Spice Lane in November, but at least it would get her off my territory. And we didn't need to talk.

So we set off down Burnmoor Crescent. I could feel her looking over her shoulder as soon as we were out of the front gate.

The people in Pebblegate think someone gets mugged every five minutes on the Spice Lane Estate. Actually, there's hardly any bother on our bit of it. The no-go area is round by the shops – but she couldn't be expected to know that.

I saw her looking at the houses. The council are doing up the whole estate. They finished Burnmoor Crescent last year.

The old houses were all crumbling pre-cast concrete, and very damp. We were moved into temporary accommodation while they did up the street. It wasn't very nice, but the new houses are beautiful, with double glazed windows, and central heating, ever so warm and comfortable.

We turned the corner into Park Rise. Half the houses there are being pulled down ready for renovation. Some of the empty ones are all boarded up. Lots have blackened windows, where the local jellyheads have lit bonfires. Burning down empty houses is quite popular around here.

'What's happened to those houses?'

I told her. She looked even more nervous.

Great, I thought, she'll really enjoy telling Amanda Brierley about Mooney Bum's wild estate. I could just see them both sniggering behind their hands.

We reached the park gates. It used to be a lovely park when I was little. Mum used to take me to play on the swings most days. But the swings have all been vandalised, and she stopped bringing Martin here after a little girl was taken to hospital when she hurt herself on a dirty needle. It's only a few idiots who spoil things on our estate. It makes me really angry, because people like the Stevensons think we're all like that.

It started to rain.

'Better get back for tea,' I said.

Except for such sparkling conversational gambits as 'Pass Lauren the salad, Hazel,' tea was a grimly silent affair. Even Martin was strangely subdued, apart from knocking his orange juice all over the table. He missed Lauren by inches. Mum had gone to enormous trouble, and cooked a fantastic low fat vegetarian pasta. She'd done a huge salad to go with it, and made a lemon mousse for pudding.

I thought Cow Features would turn her nose up at everything, but I couldn't have been more mistaken. She knocked everything back and had a second helping of pudding. In fairness I have to say Mum can be very pressing.

Straight after tea Lauren disappeared upstairs to the bathroom, and I went into the kitchen to help Mum clear up.

'Just pop upstairs and get a clean tea towel, will you, love?' she asked.

I sighed, and went slowly upstairs. Why's it always me, I thought crossly?

The airing cupboard has two doors – one in the bathroom, and one in my bedroom, which is next door.

I went into my bedroom and opened the cupboard door. In a startled moment of time I realised two things: that someone had left the opposite airing cupboard door, into the bathroom, wide open, and that Lauren was down on her knees by the loo.

And she was sticking her fingers down her throat.

For one awful, long second our eyes met.

CHAPTER FOURTEEN

I reeled backwards into my bedroom in shock. Then I heard the bolt on the bathroom door slide back. My bedroom door shot open.

Lauren marched into the room and shoved her face so close to mine our noses practically touched. Her eyes were hard and glazed. 'If you ever tell anyone about this, you're *really* dead,' she hissed.

I pushed her away from me, but she had my wrist in a painful grip. For a moment I thought she was going to hit me.

'Tell about what?' I asked stupidly. 'Let go of me – you're mad!'

Then suddenly I saw it all. She was making herself sick on purpose!

'You've got bulimia!'

The pressure on my wrist became agonising, as her nails dug in. Then suddenly she let go, and her face went all wrong. She dropped onto her knees, her body wracked with hard and painful sobs.

It was weird, but in that moment I felt all the hatred bottled tight inside me drain away. I sat down on the bed beside her. Oh God, I must do this right! I tried hard to think about the training I'd been given at school as a mediator. I put a hand awkwardly on her shoulder. She shook it off angrily.

'I don't want your pity!' she gasped.

I sat quietly until her sobs subsided a little. Then I went into the bathroom and tore some sheets of toilet paper off the roll. I gave them to her silently.

There's nothing worse than knowing you've got great green slimy ribbons hanging down from your nose.

She blew her nose and wiped her face. 'Thanks.' She was breathing more normally now.

'Look, Lauren,' I began awkwardly, 'you can get help, you know. It's nothing to be ashamed of. Lots of famous people have had bulimia!'

A ghost of a smile flickered on her lips for a moment.

'And of course I won't say a word to anyone

about it – but you really should tell someone – your Mum and Dad, or the doctor.'

Lauren grimaced. 'It's all right for you, Hazel. You don't know my parents. They're not the sort of people you can talk to. You don't know how lucky you are to have parents like yours.'

'What do you mean?'

'Your Mum and Dad are so...nice, and kind, and...friendly.' She blinked hard. 'And they really love you...anyone can see that!' She started to cry again.

'I'm sure your parents love you, Lauren. They must be so proud of you.'

Lauren rubbed her nose angrily. 'That's just it, *proud*; love doesn't come into it. I've got to be perfect all the time – in top sets for everything, "the Best Young Dancer in the Midlands", always well groomed and polite. Forget love - they just want to show off about me to everyone. I hate them, Hazel, I really hate them!'

I felt lost for words for a moment.

'And you've no idea what it's been like at home since I got suspended – they didn't speak to me for three days, I wasn't allowed out of the house, and then there was this big talk about the disgrace I'd brought on the whole family. Then Dad said he wasn't sure if he could ever love me again!' Lauren's voice shook.

'That's cruel, Lauren, really cruel!' I burst out. 'But I expect he didn't mean it – people say awful things sometimes when they're really angry.'

'You don't know my dad.' Lauren gave a deep shudder and sat down properly on the bed beside me.

'Can you talk to your Mum?' I asked.

'Not really – Dad says I mustn't bother her – she's got a really demanding job, and she works such long hours she's tired out when she gets home.'

'Oh.' I didn't feel I was getting very far.

'I'll be all right.' Lauren stood up. 'Perhaps we should go downstairs – your mum must be wondering what's happened to us.'

'Oh – she'll just think we've been making friends.'

I clasped my hand to my mouth, suddenly aware of what I had said.

'Well.' Lauren looked at me for a moment, then shrugged. 'Perhaps we have – sort of!'

CHAPTER FIFTEEN

'Can I talk to you, please, Hazel?'

It was Tuesday – the day Leanne and I are on duty as mediators. We were just walking past the library when this tiny kid with enormous specs tugged at my sleeve.

'Yes, of course! Shall we go somewhere a bit quieter?'

The boy nodded. Then I realised who he was.

'Aren't you Sital's brother?' asked Leanne

He nodded shyly.

We went to the little room that's been set to one side for the use of the mediators. I set out three chairs for us.

'Is there anything troubling you, Ram?'

He was twisting his shoe round and round on the carpet as if he was hoping to dig it up.

'Has someone been bullying you, Ram?'

Leanne smiled encouragingly at him.

Another silent nod.

'Do you want to talk about it, Ram?'

He shook his head miserably. This mediation business was hard work sometimes!

'You know, we can't help you unless you tell us what's wrong,' I said gently.

Beads of sweat glistened on Ram's forehead. Then he looked up, his eyes desperate. 'There's this kid in our class who won't leave me alone.'

'What's he doing, Ram?'

'I can't read too good. I get stuck sometimes, and whenever I have to read out in class he's always sniggering and saying nasty things.'

'What does he say?'

'Oh – you know – he calls me names like "Thicko" and sometimes he calls me "Four Eyes" and much ruder things – I don't like to say.'

'Does he do anything else?' asked Leanne gently.

'He's always messing with my things; like, he threw my bag round the classroom, and got all the other kids to hide it. And he called me a wimp when I got upset.'

'That's really horrible, and you were quite right

to tell us about it Ram,' I said. 'What's his name?'

Ram hung his head. His right foot bored deeper into the carpet.

'I know it's hard, Ram, but we really need to know his name – otherwise we can't help you.'

'It's Jason,' he muttered.

'Jason who?' I said patiently.

'Jason Byrne.'

'Well done, Ram,' I said. 'You've been really brave. Now, if you like, we can all get together, and talk about it.'

Ram didn't look very happy about that.

'OK,' he said slowly, 'only – only I don't want anyone else to know…you won't tell Sital, will you? Or anyone else in my class?'

'No way, Ram,' said Leanne. 'Anything you tell us is confidential – and of course we won't say a word to Sital.'

Ram gave us a wobbly smile, relief written all over his face. 'Thanks Hazel, thanks Leanne.' And he was gone.

This sort of thing has been happening a lot recently. Quite often it's fairly little things, that we feel confident we can sort out, but sometimes it's more complicated and then we call in a teacher.

It's been strange since Lauren and I reached our truce – if that's what you can call it. She's been so quiet and subdued since she came back to school. She sort of avoids me, as if she's embarrassed or something. But I know what's going on inside Lauren, and the knowledge scares me; I know that she's in deep trouble, and that she should be getting proper help. The thing is, I can't do anything about it. I've promised her I won't tell, and she doesn't want my help. I think Leanne and Jenny have sussed out that something's happened between Lauren and me, but they haven't said anything.

And another thing, Lauren doesn't hang around with Amanda Brierley like she used to – I think Lauren's parents and maybe the school must have tried to break up the friendship. So now Amanda has no one; apart from Lauren, she's never had many friends. She was never really nasty to me, and I think that without Lauren she'd have been all right. So suddenly I am finding myself feeling sorry for her – I know what it's like to be lonely. I try to be friendly towards her, but she sort of pulls away. I think deep down, she's quite shy.

It's only three weeks to Christmas now, and everyone's started to get excited. Year Nine are putting on an end of term show, and I've offered to help with the costumes. It's all a bit frantic, because I'm in the middle of trying to make a Spiderman costume for Martin. The trousers and top weren't too difficult – I adapted a pyjama pattern – but I'm having real difficulties with the mask.

It was Design the afternoon after I'd spoken to Ram.

'Oy, Hazel!' It was Michael Evans. 'You know I'm being Buttons in the Christmas Sketch?'

'Uh-huh.'

'I don't suppose you'd help out with my costume? My mum's useless, and needlework's not my strong point!'

'What is?' said Jenny cheekily.

'My wit and charm are famous throughout the school,' said Michael airily.

Amongst the laughter that followed this modest statement, I said, 'I'll help you out, Michael, if you can think of a way of making a mask for Spiderman!'

'You're on, I'll bend my creative genius to it!' Michael gave a mock bow.

We settled down to work. I took Spiderman's trousers over to the machine to turn up the legs. Lauren was sitting by herself moodily pinning two pieces of fabric.

'Hi,' I said awkwardly.

She glared at me, and for a moment I thought she was going to bite my head off.

'Are you doing anything in the show?' I asked gingerly.

'Nope. I've got a big dancing competition coming up. Mum says I've got to save all my energies for that.'

For a moment she looked right at me. I was startled by the deep misery in her eyes.

'Don't you want to do it?'

'What I want doesn't matter,' said Lauren savagely.

'Just tell them, if you really hate doing it,' I said, appalled.

'I've told you, you just don't know my parents!'

Lauren jabbed a pin into the fabric viciously and caught her finger. I suddenly noticed how thin and frail her arms were. She was wearing a baggy sweatshirt, and her wrist stuck out of the cuff like a sparrow's leg. A tear rolled down her face and dripped onto the fabric.

I could think of nothing to say.

CHAPTER SIXTEEN

Only two more weeks to Christmas!

I was sitting on the floor putting the finishing touches to Martin's Spiderman costume. Mum had sent him to bed early because he's got a bad cold. Michael Evans came up with this brilliant idea for the mask: he worked out a design in fabric dyes and I transferred it onto some stretch fabric. Mrs Parsons helped with the tricky bits. It looks dead good.

Mum was waltzing around the room with the vacuum cleaner. She's looking pretty classy these days. She's lost nine pounds, and has a new colour on her hair. It's astonishing – she looks years younger – not like my mum at all. And she's got so much energy, and laughs a lot more. I caught her having a go on Martin's scooter last week!

I've lost twelve pounds. Mum's going to take

me to town to buy some new clothes when I break the stone barrier. And I feel so much better, too. OK, so I doubt I'll ever be really skinny – who wants to be, anyway? – but I caught sight of myself in the mirror the other day, and I thought, 'Hmm...not bad, Hazel, not bad!' Suddenly there were curves appearing in some of the right places!

As I sat on the floor, remembering that image in the mirror, I was off into a very pleasant daydream...

SCENE: *The Pioneer Camp Farewell Disco*
(I float into the hall in a brand new slinky, black silk dress.)

ANDY: *(His head turning as he sees me across the room.) Hazel! Is it really you? You look gorgeous!*

ME: *Thanks, Andy! (A spotlight falls on me and I dance as I never have before—)*

Hazel! Really! Get a grip on yourself! I jolted myself back to reality blushing furiously.

Suddenly the phone rang.

'I'll get it,' said Mum. 'Oh, hello, Mrs Stevenson!'

I pricked up my ears.

'No, she's not here, I'm afraid.'

Pause.

'Yes, of course, we'll let you know if she turns up here.'

Pause.

'Mmm. I agree – I think I'd call the police if she doesn't turn up in the next hour…'

Pause.

'Still, you know teenage girls – perhaps she's gone late-night shopping, and hasn't told you. I'm sure she'll turn up in a bit. Uh-huh. OK, take care.'

Mum came into the living room looking troubled.

'Lauren didn't come home after school, today – her parents are worried sick.'

'Perhaps she's gone round to Amanda Brierley's,' I suggested.

'No – they've contacted the Brierleys already.'

'Oh well, she's got her head screwed on, has Lauren. She knows how to look after herself.'

Then I had a sudden thought. 'Have they tried

to get her on her mobile?'

'No – that's the funny thing – she didn't take it with her.'

Suddenly I felt uneasy. It was strange; as I was growing in confidence and happiness, Lauren seemed to have been fading away. Day by day I have seen her getting skinnier; only skinny isn't really the right word.

She's beginning to look more like a skeleton.

She doesn't look like beautiful, healthy Lauren any more. She seems to have lost her sparkle.

The odd thing is, no one else seems to have noticed. She's very good at hiding herself under layers and layers of clothes…only I *know*.

When I got to school on Wednesday morning there was no Lauren. Amanda Brierley came over to me.

'She didn't go home last night, Hazel. Her dad phoned the police and then he came round to our house to see if I had any idea where she might be.'

I imagined Mr Stevenson driving round the dark streets looking for his daughter.

A red-haired girl stuck her head round the door. 'Can Hazel Mooney and Amanda Brierley go to Mr Edwards's office straight away, please!'

'Off you go,' said Miss Kennedy. She looked very serious.

What now, I thought?

When we got to Mr Edwards's room there was a policewoman there.

'Sit down, girls,' said Mr Edwards quietly. 'Police Sergeant Collins has a few questions to ask you. I believe you know that Lauren Stevenson is missing from home?'

We both nodded.

Sergeant Collins turned to Amanda first. 'As Lauren's best friend, we wondered if Lauren has said anything to you that might help us, Amanda. Has she ever talked of running away from home?'

Amanda shook her head. 'She doesn't talk to me much these days. She's been ever so quiet since – since she was in that bit of trouble.' Her eyes slid nervously in my direction.

'What about you, Hazel,' said Mr Edwards.

'She never talked about running away, Sir – but, well, she's not been very happy lately.'

'Can you tell us a bit more?'

I hesitated. It didn't seem right to betray Lauren's confidence.

'I really need your help here, Hazel,' said Sergeant Collins. 'If we're to find Lauren.'

Suddenly I realised that I had to tell them something.

'Well, she has told me she doesn't get on very well with her mum and dad, and there's this dance competition coming up. She really didn't want to do it, Sir, only her mum and dad were making her.'

'It's true,' Amanda nodded.

'I see.' Mr Edwards looked very thoughtful. 'Thank you, Hazel, that's a big help.'

'Did she mention any other problems to you, Hazel?' asked Sergeant Collins. 'Or did she have a boyfriend, say, that her mum and dad don't know about? Anything you can remember could be really helpful.'

'I don't think there was anyone, Miss.'

I tried hard to remember. And then I thought: should I tell them about the bulimia? But I'd promised not to... How would she ever trust me again, if I betrayed her now? No, I couldn't do that.

'Well, that's all, girls,' said Mr Edwards. 'If you do remember anything at all, no matter how silly it seems, come and tell me straight away.'

We left the room.

Of course everyone talked about it all day.

There was still no news when I got home from school that night.

Mum shoved the *Leicester Gazette* into my hands as I walked through the door. There was a black and white photo of Lauren – very bad – on the first page. I read:

LOCAL GIRL MISSING

Police are concerned for the safety of fourteen-year-old schoolgirl Lauren Stevenson. Lauren failed to return from school yesterday, on 12 December and has not been seen since. Lauren is five feet seven tall, of slim build, and has long blonde hair. She was wearing a large, black jacket, grey school skirt, white shirt and black fringed boots. She was carrying a black shoulder bag with distinctive silver stripe. If you have seen Lauren, or have any information about her whereabouts, please phone Market Street Police Station on 01172 545151.

I sat down on the telephone table in the hall. My legs had suddenly gone wobbly.

We were all rather subdued that evening. I got ratty with Martin for no real reason. He saw *Toy Story 2* on video last week, so now he thinks he's Buzz Lightyear. He keeps leaping off the sofa shouting, 'To infinity and beyond!' Normally it would have made me laugh, but he caught my ankle painfully as he crash-landed.

'Pack it in, Martin!' I bellowed.

He looked all hurt.

'That was my falling with style,' he said indignantly.

'Isn't it time he went to bed, Mum?' I griped.

'You're not my friend any more!' Martin stomped out of the room in a huff.

There are definitely moments when Martin can be a real pain.

'I expect there'll be some news soon, Hazel,' said Mum gently. She didn't sound very convinced.

Later on Leanne phoned. She said someone had spotted a girl who looked like Lauren walking along the canal towpath on Raylestone Meadows.

There have been two horrible murders on the canal towpath. A girl was assaulted there only a few months ago.

That night I laid in bed and thought. One horrible picture after another presented itself to my mind's eye.

Lauren alone, sleeping rough somewhere.

Lauren lying face down in the icy black canal.

A car cruising slowly along the road. Stopping. A man leaping out, grabbing Lauren and bundling her into the back.

And I couldn't stop feeling that somehow I was to blame. If Lauren hadn't been suspended, her parents wouldn't have been so angry with her… If only I had found the right words to say to her that day in my bedroom, or when she was crying in Design. If only I had spoken to someone about her illness.

If only.

I couldn't sleep, that night.

CHAPTER SEVENTEEN

First thing on Thursday morning I went to the staff room in search of Miss Kennedy.

'I've got something important to tell you, Miss.' The words came out in a rush. I was not looking forward to it. The sooner said the better.

'Is it about Lauren?'

'Yes.' Suddenly I felt breathless.

'Take your time, Hazel.' Miss Kennedy smiled encouragingly.

'The day Lauren came to my house to apologise – about – you know – I saw her in the bathroom after tea. She was putting her fingers down her throat, trying to make herself sick. She suffers from bulimia!'

For a moment Miss Kennedy stood in startled silence. Then she put her arm around my shoulders and whirled me off down the corridor to the head's office.

'Well done, Hazel – you've done the right thing to tell someone. Now I want you to be really brave, and tell Mr Edwards everything you've told me.'

For a few horrible moments I stood outside the head's door while Miss Kennedy talked to him.

Then the door opened and Mr Edwards called 'Come on in, Hazel,' in a friendly voice.

'Miss Kennedy has told me that you think Lauren may be suffering from an eating disorder, Hazel.'

I nodded. 'Yes, Sir. Bulimia, Sir.' And I told him what I had seen in our bathroom. And about how thin she'd become. I told him everything.

'Does anyone else know about this?'

'No, Sir.'

'Why ever didn't you tell someone before?'

'I promised I wouldn't, Sir.'

Mr Edwards sighed. 'There are good promises and bad promises, Hazel.'

I felt confused.

'Normally it's important to keep a promise, but if someone's life's in danger, or serious harm could result from your silence, then it's even more important to tell a responsible adult.'

I nodded silently. What an idiot I'd been.

'But at least you've done the right thing in telling me now, Hazel. I'll phone Lauren's parents straight away. And of course, the police will have to be informed, in case…in view of her frame of mind.'

He nodded to me to leave the room, and picked up the phone. I felt about as big as a microchip.

The rest of the day passed slowly and miserably. Contradictory rumours about Lauren abounded.

'I hear they're dragging the canal down by King's Lock,' said Michael Evans at break.

'*Michael!*' Leanne froze him with a look. 'That's just a silly rumour! They found out that the girl spotted down by the canal last night was Kerry Pearson in 9T. She could easily be mistaken for Lauren from a distance.'

'How do you know?' I asked.

'Because her mum met my mum at the doctor's last night. The police had been round their house checking.'

'Oh,' I said. Everyone seemed to know more than me. At least Lauren hadn't drowned in the canal.

Suddenly I noticed that Amanda Brierley was hanging on to Leanne's every word. She had gone very pale. I went over and sat next to her.

'I'm sure she'll be all right, Amanda,' I said awkwardly, trying to convince myself as much as her.

Amanda nodded and blew her nose hard.

I struggled to say something more but I was feeling a bit tearful myself. And then, just in the nick of time, before I started bawling, Jenny came over to us.

'Come on, Amanda,' she said, putting an arm round her shoulder. 'Why don't we all go outside for a bit – it's stuffy in here.'

I gave Jenny a grateful smile as we left the classroom.

As I walked home from school that afternoon an icy wind whirled the crisp packets and cigarette butts around the pavements. There was that strange smell in the air that comes before snow. Heavy grey clouds scudded across the sky, and a coldness gripped my stomach that had nothing to do with the weather.

After tea we all sat round the telly watching *Eastward News*. Of course, Mum and Dad and

I were talking about Lauren. We were all very subdued – even Martin sensed something was wrong, and sat playing quietly with Buzz and Woody.

There was an item about a factory fire, and then a photo of Lauren flashed onto the screen.

Instant silence.

'There is still no news of missing schoolgirl, Lauren Stevenson.' It was Maggie White, one of the *Eastward* newscasters. 'It is now two days since Lauren went missing, and police are concerned for her safety. Lauren left Alderman Newbold High School in the Spice Lane area of Leicester at three-thirty on Tuesday afternoon, and has not been seen since. We have Lauren's parents, Mr and Mrs Stevenson, with us in the studio now, to make an appeal.'

Suddenly the cameras switched to the Stevensons. Mrs Stevenson was gazing at the floor, her hands gripped tightly together. Mr Stevenson looked terribly old. His voice quavered as he spoke.

'Lauren, if you are watching this, please get in touch. You're not in trouble, we just want to know you're safe. We...we love you very much, so if you're out there, please let us know you're all right.'

His shoulders had started to shake, and Mum leaned across and switched off the telly. We were all upset.

I ran upstairs to my bedroom. I felt I needed to be on my own for a bit. I went over to the window without putting on the light. Underneath the orange glow of the street lamps a thin layer of snow had settled. I thought, it's strange how snow has the power to change a place. Everywhere looked so clean, so still, so new, it was as if the world had just been made for me alone.

Then my stomach lurched as I thought of Lauren out there, lying in a doorway somewhere, hungry and shivering.

Where do you go, when you want no one to find you? I thought. London? Possibly – the city where the streets are paved with gold. That's where most runaways make for. But maybe the best place to hide is right under the noses of the people you want to escape – the last place anyone would think of looking. I thought of my week in the garage, of my need to be somewhere alone, away from cruel tongues and prying eyes. They say a sick animal always finds a dark place to hide.

Suddenly I had it!

Why hadn't I thought of it before?

I ran downstairs and grabbed my jacket from the hall. I was out of the door before anyone had time to stop me.

'Back in a minute, Mum!' I yelled. Then I was pounding down the street, skidding in the wet snow, heading towards the park. Lauren's words that awful wet November afternoon hammered in my head. 'What's happened to those houses?'

I turned the corner into Park Rise. Where should I begin? Most of the houses were boarded up. I must be systematic, I thought, and check each one in turn.

I was out of breath now, with a bad stitch in my side. I doubled up for a minute to relieve it and looked at the first house in the street. Its windows were heavily boarded, the gate hanging off its hinges, and there was a burned-out car in the front garden.

In the light of the sodium lamps I could see my way round to the back of the house. The back door had gone, and for a moment I didn't think I could face going into the dark mouth of the doorway. Why hadn't I waited to get a torch?

I knew from the plan of our house that I must be in the kitchen, and I stretched out my hands to feel my way around. There was an awful smell of damp and dirt, and nastiness. Then something small scurried over my foot and I screamed and shot out of the back door.

This was no good. What I ought to do was go back home, tell Mum and Dad and get help.

But I didn't want to do that. I wanted to find Lauren on my own.

Perhaps I wanted to make up for the fact that I hadn't had the sense to tell someone at school about Lauren's illness sooner – about how unhappy and unwell she was, before she started to go really downhill and maybe...

Stop it, stop it! This wasn't helping anyone!

Think.

If Lauren was hiding in one of these houses, wouldn't there be some little sign, some clue to show she was there?

Fire! Surely she would have made herself some sort of fire to survive?

I walked back to the street and scanned the skyline for any sign of smoke. Nothing. Down at the bottom of the road, near the park gates, a gang of lads was hanging around a motorbike. I prayed they wouldn't see me.

There was nothing for it. I would have to walk round all the empty houses and look for signs of life.

A light! That was it. She must have brought a torch with her, or at least a few candles.

I set off down the next garden path, and checked the outside of the house.

Nothing.

I stepped over the little fence dividing it from its neighbour and stopped dead in my tracks.

There were fresh footprints in the snow. They wandered around the garden, and then led back into the house. I groped my way into the kitchen and into the hall.

'Lauren?' I tried to make my voice steady.

Then I smelled something – the unmistakable tang of candle fat. It was coming from upstairs. I felt my way up the stairs, my breath coming in gasps. Suppose it wasn't Lauren? Supposing it was a drunk, or a tramp?

Then I saw the ring of light above me, and peering over the upstairs bannisters, a white face, with huge dark eyes.

'Oh Lauren, thank God I've found you.'

It was me who burst into tears.

CHAPTER EIGHTEEN

I stood outside the W.R.V.S shop in the foyer of the Leicester Royal Hospital, gazing at the huge bunches of balloons bobbing in the draught from the doors like crazy aerial flowers. Which one should I choose?

There were gaudy parrots, silver dolphins, huge brilliantly-coloured butterflies, laughing fish, and crimson valentine hearts. I liked the look of the dolphin, but it had 'Happy Birthday!' written all over it, so that was no good. Eventually, after rejecting a parrot that said 'You're irresistible!' I settled for a gold and blue butterfly that simply read 'Get Well Soon!'

It was three days since I had found Lauren. My mind flicked back to the moment when I saw her standing at the top of the stairs. I had been so desperate to do everything right this time. I followed Lauren into the bedroom where she had been living. She didn't say anything, just sank down onto a dirty mattress on the floor. Then I saw that she was shaking with the cold, so I took off my jacket and wrapped it round her. There were no covers on the bed, just an old pair of curtains she'd got from somewhere for blankets. A candle flickered in an empty milk bottle, throwing a circle of light onto a collection of empty cans and chocolate wrappers. Monstrous shadows ballooned and shrank as the flame wavered in the draught from the door. Wallpaper hung down from the walls in damp ribbons, and where the plaster was bare you could see inky streaks and blotches of mildew. It smelled.

I knelt down by Lauren. She was so light and fragile the candlelight seemed almost to shine through her. She was curled tightly on the mattress, like a baby before it's born. She did not seem to be able to speak.

This time I knew what to do. I switched on my mobile. Oh sugar – just when I really needed it my battery was flat! I thought quickly.

'Listen Lauren,' I said gently. 'You're very ill. I'm going to get help, and I'll be back in a minute.'

I didn't like leaving her for a second in the state she was in, but I knew she needed urgent medical help. I pulled the curtains over her again and picked my way cautiously down the dark well of the staircase.

There was a phone box by the park. I slipped and slithered down the street. Thank goodness the phone box was working. With frozen fingers I dialled 999.

'Emergency. Which service?'

'Ambulance and police, please,' I said breathlessly. I gave the address of the house where I had found Lauren, and then made my way back up the street. Almost before I'd reached the house the first police car arrived, and then an ambulance.

There were so many people all over the place I can't quite remember what happened next, except that Lauren was carried downstairs by two paramedics and whipped away to the hospital. I found myself surrounded by the police, explaining everything.

A policewoman drove me home, and then I had to face Mum and Dad. I thought I was going to get a real roasting, but in all the excitement, they forgot to tell me off for running out into the dark night alone. Everyone made a great fuss of me and kept saying, 'Well done, Hazel!'

It was a strange evening, because people were treating me as if I was some sort of heroine, but everything seemed unreal, and all I could see in my mind's eye was that squalid candlelit room, and Lauren curled up on the filthy mattress.

And now here I was coming to visit her in hospital. She was so ill that no one except her parents was allowed to be with her for the first week. Later we found out that she was suffering from dehydration and hypothermia. Then this morning in school Mr Edwards sent for me, and said Lauren's parents had asked if I would like to go and see her. We all made her a giant get-well card, and everyone signed it. The balloon was my idea.

I made my way to ward twenty-eight in the lift, and went to the nurses' desk.

'I've come to see Lauren Stevenson,' I said shyly. Now that the moment had come, I wondered what on earth I was going to say to her.

'She's in a side ward – we're keeping her quiet

at the moment. I'm Lauren's named nurse Sarah – I'll take you to see her if you like.'

The nurse led the way down the corridor. With only five days to go to Christmas the ward was bright with decorations and balloons. Ward twenty-eight was a children's ward – very busy, and noisy, so I could see why they had put Lauren by herself. A little boy with an arm in plaster scooted by on a tricycle, and a group of older children were making paper chains with a play leader.

We turned a corner into a quiet bay. Nurse Sarah stuck her head into a little single room. 'A visitor for you, Lauren,' she smiled.

'Hi,' I said shyly.

Lauren was sitting up in bed, her long, fair hair clean and shining. But she was thin – really, really thin. I was shocked for a moment. Without her layers of baggy clothes every bone stood out. How come none of us had *really* noticed how much she'd changed? My mind slipped back to Pioneer Camp, to Lauren abseiling lightly down the wall and doing her famous 'star', healthy, slim, and beautiful. How could we all have been so stupid not to see the seriousness of what was happening in front of our eyes, even me with the knowledge I had?

Then I realised that Lauren was smiling at me. I hoped she hadn't been able to read what was in my mind.

'I've brought you a card from everyone at school.' I held it out to her. 'And this is from me!' I gave her the butterfly.

'Thanks.' She fumbled awkwardly with the string.

'I'll tie the butterfly on the end of the bed, if you like,' I offered. 'Otherwise it might take off!'

We both laughed a little awkwardly, but the butterfly had broken the ice, and suddenly we were much more relaxed.

I sat on the end of the bed while she undid her card. Everyone had signed it, and lots of people had written little messages as well. For a moment I saw her eyes fill with tears.

We sat chatting for a little while, laughing over Michael Evans's latest awful joke:

Doctor, doctor, I've lost my memory.

When did it happen?

When did what happen?

Lauren's nurse stuck her head round the door

and startled us. 'Time for your mid-afternoon drink, Lauren!' She held out a glass of pale pink liquid.

Lauren pulled a face.

'Cheer up – it's strawberry this time!' She laughed at Lauren's expression.

'Can't be as bad as chicken flavour, I suppose.' Lauren drank it down as fast as she could.

'Good girl,' said the nurse approvingly. I noticed she watched to make sure it all disappeared. Then she smiled at me. 'I think Lauren's had long enough for her first visit, now. You can come back tomorrow and stay longer if you want.'

'Can I just have another minute, please?' begged Lauren. 'On my own.'

'Just one minute, then.' We were alone again.

'Hazel, I want to say thank you for finding me the other night.'

I blushed furiously. I had hoped we weren't going to get round to all of that.

'Oh Lauren, you don't have to thank me! I feel so bad about it all – if you hadn't got into trouble because of me, it would probably never have happened.'

Lauren shook her head. 'It wasn't anything to do with you, Hazel. It was me. I felt so bad inside – like I was going to explode, and all the anger burst out of me... And I hated my parents, hated everyone and – I know this sounds quite mad but – jeering at you made me feel better. You see, I really think, no, thought *I* was fat...'

'You, *fat* !' I said incredulously.

'I know...it's mad, isn't it? And there's still a little bit of me that's afraid I might be, and ugly and repulsive too... And throwing up all the time, that made me feel so good – like *I* was in control, not my parents. You get sort of hooked on it...in the end I couldn't stop.'

'But still, I should have told someone how ill you were, then you would have got some help.'

'I've had a long talk with a counsellor, Hazel. I told her everything – about how Mum and Dad were never off my back, pushing me to be the best all the time. And how I never felt they really loved me for myself. And – and I told her about what Dad said, after – after I was suspended... That was the worst bit, you know, Hazel.'

I nodded, appalled at the memory.

'Then the counsellor talked to Mum and Dad for ages, and then we all talked together. Mum said she was really sorry she wasn't there for me when I needed her, and Dad said that he really believed that by pushing me so hard he was doing his best for me…and he said he was sorry, really sorry for what he'd said, he didn't mean it…and, well, we all had a good cry.' Lauren blew her nose hard.

'You know, when I was in the garage, hiding from everyone, I felt just like you did, Lauren,' I said slowly. 'I felt no one else in the world was as unlovable as me.'

And I thought of myself crying in the dark, cold garage, and Lauren shivering on the dirty mattress, alone in that awful house. And of all the kids at school who'd been bullied, all of us thinking we were the only ones, feeling pathetic, afraid to tell anyone else what we were going through. All shut away in our own dark little rooms.

'Haven't you two finished gossiping yet?' It was named nurse Sarah again. 'I don't know, you young girls – chatter, chatter, chatter. What wouldn't I give to be young again!'

I caught Lauren's eye.

Her mouth twitched, and then suddenly we were both shaking and gasping with laughter.

WEL, U HAV 2 LAF OR UO CRII

Transcriptions of the text messages:

Text message p19:
Lauren Stevenson to Amanda Brierley

What do you call a Hazel in a heatwave? Roast pork!
Got to go now, parents are watching, twenty-four hours a day, seven days a week!
See you,
Lauren

Text message p29:
Lauren Stevenson to Amanda Brierley

Are you free to talk? I'm exhausted - because of more dance practice. I hate it! Glad you're going to camp.
Have you heard? The Pig's going too.
Nightmare!
Got to go now.
Parents are watching, as per usual.
Lauren

Text message p40:
Lauren Stevenson to Amanda Brierley

Once upon a time, there were three pigs, Mummy
Pig, Daddy Pig, and Hazel Pig.
Did you see Hazel's mother this morning?
She's got a snout just like Hazel's!
Laughing my head off,
Lauren

Text message p54:
Lauren Stevenson to Amanda Brierley

Are you free to talk?
You should have seen the Pig's face when she came
down the wall!
I was rolling on the floor laughing!
See you,
Lauren

Text message in response p55:
Amanda Brierley to Lauren:

I wish I'd been there! And have you seen her top?
Gross!
Got to go now,
Amanda

Text message p75:
Lauren Stevenson to Hazel Mooney

What's pink and black and wobbles?
A pig in a maternity dress!

Text message p89:
Lauren Stevenson to Hazel Mooney

Hi Pig. So where are you hiding?
You're on your own now. Just you wait – you can't
escape me.

Text message p :
Lauren Stevenson to Hazel Mooney

Hi Pig.
What, still alive?

Text message p92:
Lauren Stevenson to Hazel Mooney

Die Pig, die.

Glossary of other abbreviations:

p45 GTT – Good to talk

If you are worried about any of the problems faced by the girls in **Hazel, Not a Nut,** there are lots of places you can go to for help.

For advice and information on Eating Disorders and related conditions:
This includes disorders such as Bulimia and Anorexia, as well as problems such as being over or underweight and overeating

- **For advice and support, for sufferers and those around them:**

Eating Disorders Association
www.edauk.com
1st Floor, Wensum House
103 Prince of Wales Road
Norwich
NR1 1DW
Information line: 01603 619 090
Helpline (8.30-20.30 weekdays, 13.00-16.30 Sat): 0845 634 1414
Youthline for up to 18-years-old (16.00-18.30 weekdays, 13.00-16.30 Sat): 0845 634 7650
Email: info@edauk.com

National Centre for Eating Disorders
www.eating-disorders.org.uk
54 New Road
Esher
Surrey
KT10 9NU
01372 469 493
ncfed@globalnet.co.uk
They can also put you in touch with
counsellors and support groups local to you.

Childline
www.childline.org.uk/eatingproblems.asp
Helpline: 0800 1111

- **For specific information on Eating Disorders, for sufferers and those around them:**

NHS website
For further information on definitions, causes,
symptoms and treatment of different Eating
Disorders, and for links to contacts and
useful websites.
www.equip.nhs.uk/topics/neuro/eating.html

British Nutrition Foundation

Their site advises on healthy eating and ways in which a well-balanced and sensible diet can help in your overall wellbeing.
www.nutrition.org.uk

For advice and information on Bullying:

- **For advice and support, for victims and their friends, family and schools:**

Careline
Cardinal Heenan Centre
326 High Road
Ilford
IG1 1QP
020 8514 1177
They provide telephone counselling for those being bullied, or facing any other problems.

Anti-Bullying Campaign (ABC)
Helpline (term time: Mon-Fri 10.00-16.00,

during holidays: Mon, Weds and Fri
10.00-16.00): 020 7378 1446
Provides advice for victims, as well as for the
bullies themselves – on how they can break
their bullying habits. They also produce free
information booklets that they will send to you
on request, as well as advise on counsellors and
support groups local to individuals.

Bullying Online
www.bullying.co.uk
You can email someone for support and advice
24 hours-a-day, 365 days-a-year at:
help@bullying.co.uk

Childline
www.childline.org.uk/bullying.asp
Helpline: 0800 1111

Samaritans
www.samaritans.org
08457 90 90 90
jo@samaritans.org is online to deal with your
bullying worries and queries

*

- **For specific information on bullying, for victims and their friends, family and schools:**

BBC
The BBC's website has an informative page on bullying, particularly bullying in schools, featuring discussions, advice and information.
www.bbc.co.uk/school/bullying
The BBC's website also has a detailed and fun-filled page on healthy eating, featuring easy recipes, question-and-answer sessions with famous chefs and a resident nutritionist, as well as fact sheets and advice pages.
www.bbc.co.uk/food/healthyeating

NSPCC
www.there4me.com
Here you can talk to counsellors in real time about anything, including bullying and eating disorders.

More Black Apples for you to get your teeth into...

1 84121 437 X   £4.99

BALLOON HOUSE
By Brian Keaney

When Neve was a child, her father used to make
up special stories for her about the magic
Balloon House. But it's hard to recapture this
intimacy now that he's moved away and remarried.
Neve is determined not to like her father's new
family. But then danger explodes into Neve's
life, calling on her deeper feelings of love and loyalty.
Trust in her father and their shared memories may
be the only way to survive.

'Thoughtful and exciting.' *Books for Keeps*

1 84121 530 9   £4.99

FAMILY SECRETS
By Brian Keaney

Kate's mother, Anne, has a past full of secrets. Why did she leave her home in Ireland before Kate was born? Why does she never speak to Kate's grandmother? And why does she never mention Kate's father? Now Anne and Kate are making the long journey back to the west coast of Ireland where Kate's grandmother is seriously ill in hospital. Will Kate find out about her father and solve the mystery of her mother's silence?

ORCHARD BLACK APPLES

All priced at £4.99

Orchard Black Apples are available from all good bookshops,
or can be ordered direct from the publisher:
Orchard Books, PO BOX 29, Douglas IM99 1BQ
Credit card orders please telephone 01624 836000
or fax 01624 837033
or visit our Internet site: www.wattspub.co.uk
or e-mail: bookshop@enterprise.net for details.

To order please quote title, author and ISBN
and your full name and address.
Cheques and postal orders should be made payable to 'Bookpost plc.'
Postage and packing is FREE within the UK
(overseas customers should add £1.00 per book)

Prices and availability are subject to change.

1 84121 005 6 £4.99

BITTER FRUIT
By Brian Keaney

Rebecca's dad is always moaning. One night Rebecca
has had enough. She tells him she hates him.
And these are the last words she will ever say to him.
Grief at her father's death is mixed with terrible guilt.
And while Rebecca is trying to cope with these
powerful emotions she discovers that her father
had a terrible secret, and suddenly life becomes
unbearably complicated. Now Rebecca must learn to
face tragedy...and the truth.

'A gripping read.' *Sugar*

SHORTLISTED FOR THE ANGUS AWARD

1 84121 858 8   £4.99

FALLING FOR JOSHUA
BY BRIAN KEANEY

Abi knows there's something special about Josh the
moment his deep blue eyes meet hers. But Abi has a
secret. And she's so used to keeping it hidden that she
can't trust him. She's been rejected before. But one
night something terrible happens and Abi's secret is
revealed. Will Josh stand by her, and will Abi learn to
accept the way she is?

'An ideal book for teenage readers.'
Times Educational Supplement